he bearer of
this scroll,

name _____

is a _____

in the Order of the Kai

The Darke Crusade

Along the walkway comes a lumbering hulk with cold scarlet eyes. This beast is covered with a vile fur which glistens in the grey-green light of the tunnel. Its long sinewy arms are outstretched and in both of its huge hands it holds chunks of dagger-like flint. Its bloated belly skims the floor as it stalks closer, and brown gluey saliva bubbles and runs freely from its fanged lower jaw.

. . . You can sense that it is being driven by a desperate hunger, a hunger that could prove stronger than your Kai mastery.

JOE DEVER was born in 1956 at Woodford Bridge in Essex. After he left college, he became a professional musician, working in studios in Europe and America. While working in Los Angeles in 1977, he discovered a game called "Dungeons and Dragons" and was soon an enthusiastic player. Five years later he won the Advanced Dungeons and Dragons Championships in the U.S., where he was the only British competitor. The award-winning Lone Wolf adventures are the culmination of many years of developing the world of Magnamund. They are printed in several languages and sold throughout the world.

BOOK 15

The Darke Crusade

Joe Dever

Illustrated by Brian Williams

Abridged Edition

BERKLEY BOOKS, NEW YORK

This role-playing novel was published in an expanded form in the
United Kingdom.

THE DARKE CRUSADE

A Berkley / Pacer Book / published by arrangement with Red Fox,
Random Century Ltd.

PRINTING HISTORY
Red Fox edition published 1991
Berkley / Pacer abridged edition / April 1993

All rights reserved.
Text copyright © 1991, 1993 by Joe Dever.
Illustrations copyright © 1991, 1993 by Brian Williams.
This book may not be reproduced in whole or in part, by
mimeograph or any other means, without permission. For
information address: Red Fox Books, 20 Vauxhall Bridge Road,
London SW1V 2SA England.

ISBN: 0-425-13798-8

Pacer is a trademark belonging to The Putnam Publishing
Corporation.

A BERKLEY BOOK ® TM 757, 375
Berkley / Pacer Books are published by The Berkley Publishing
Group,
200 Madison Avenue, New York, New York 10016.
The name "BERKLEY" and the "B" logos are trademarks
belonging to Berkley Publishing Corporation.

PRINTED IN THE UNITED STATES OF AMERICA

10 9 8 7 6 5 4 3 2

To the spirit of San Diego—America's Finest City

GRAND MASTER DISCIPLINES　　　NOTES

1	
2	
3	
4	
5	
5th Grand Master Discipline if you have completed 1 Grand Master adventure successfully	
6	
6th Grand Master Discipline if you have completed 2 Grand Master adventures successfully	

BACKPACK (max. 10 articles)	MEALS
1	
2	
3	
4	
5	—3 EP if no Meal available when instructed to eat.
6	BELT POUCH Containing Gold Crowns (50 maximum)
7	
8	
9	
10	

CS = COMBAT SKILL　EP = ENDURANCE POINTS

ACTION CHART

COMBAT SKILL	ENDURANCE POINTS
	0 = dead

COMBAT RECORD

ENDURANCE POINTS		ENDURANCE POINTS
LONE WOLF	COMBAT RATIO	ENEMY
LONE WOLF	COMBAT RATIO	ENEMY
LONE WOLF	COMBAT RATIO	ENEMY
LONE WOLF	COMBAT RATIO	ENEMY
LONE WOLF	COMBAT RATIO	ENEMY

GRAND MASTER RANK

SPECIAL ITEMS LIST

DESCRIPTION	KNOWN EFFECTS

WEAPONS LIST

WEAPONS (maximum 2 Weapons)

1	
2	

If holding Weapon and appropriate Grand Weaponmastery in combat + 5CS

GRAND WEAPONMASTERY CHECKLIST

DAGGER		SPEAR	
MACE		SHORT SWORD	
WARHAMMER		BOW	
AXE		SWORD	
QUARTERSTAFF		BROADSWORD	

QUIVER & ARROWS

Quiver	No. of arrows carried
YES/NO	

THE STORY SO FAR ...

You are Grand Master Lone Wolf, last of the Kai Lords of Sommerlund and sole survivor of a massacre that wiped out the First Order of your elite warrior caste.

It is the year MS 5076 and twenty-six years have passed since your brave kinsmen perished at the hands of the Darklords of Helgedad. These champions of evil, who were sent forth by Naar, the King of the Darkness, to destroy the fertile world of Magnamund, have themselves since been destroyed. You vowed to avenge the murder of the Kai and you kept your pledge, for it was you who brought about their downfall when alone you infiltrated their foul domain—the Darklands—and caused the destruction of their leader, Archlord Gnaag, and the seat of his power that was the infernal city of Helgedad.

In the wake of their destruction, chaos befell the Darkland armies who, until then, had been poised to conquer all of Northern Magnamund. Some factions which comprised this huge army, most notably the barbaric Drakkarim, began to fight with the others for control. This disorder quickly escalated into an all-out civil war, which allowed the freestate armies of Magnamund time in which to recover and launch a counter-offensive. Skilfully their commanders exploited the chaos and secured a swift and total victory over an enemy far superior in numbers.

For six years now peace has reigned in Sommerlund. Under your direction, the once-ruined monastery of the Kai has been thoroughly rebuilt and restored to its former glory, and the task of teaching a Second Order of Kai warriors the skills and proud traditions of your ancestors is also well under way. The new generation of Kai recruits, all of whom were born during the era of war against the Darklords, possess latent Kai skills and all show exceptional promise. These skills will be nurtured and honed to perfection during their time at the monastery so that they may teach and inspire future generations, thereby ensuring the continued security of your homeland in future years.

Your attainment of the rank of Kai Grand Master brought with it great rewards. Some, such as the restoration of the Kai and the undying gratitude of your fellow Sommlending, could have been anticipated. Yet there have also been rewards which you could not possibly have foreseen. The discovery that within you lay the potential to develop Kai Disciplines beyond those of the Magnakai, which, until now, were thought to be the ultimate that a Kai Master could aspire to, was truly a revelation. Your discovery has inspired you to set out upon a new and previously unknown path in search of the wisdom and power that no Kai lord before you has ever possessed. In the name of your creator, the God Kai, and for the greater glory of Sommerlund and the Goddess Ishir, you have vowed to reach the very pinnacle of Kai perfection— to attain all of the Grand Master Disciplines and become the first Kai Supreme Master.

With diligence and determination you set about the restoration of the Kai monastery and organized the training of the Second Order recruits. Your efforts were soon rewarded and, within the space of two short years, the first raw recruits had graduated to become a cadre of gifted Kai Masters who, in turn, were able to commence the teaching of their skills to subsequent intakes of Kai novices. Readily the Kai Masters rose to their new-found responsibilities, leaving you free to devote more of your time to the pursuit and perfection of the Grand Master Disciplines. During this period you also received expert tutelage in the ways of magic from two of your most trusted friends and advisors: Guildmaster Banedon, leader of the Brotherhood of the Crystal Star, and Lord Rimoah, speaker for the High Council of the Elder Magi.

In the deepest subterranean level of the monastery, one hundred feet below the Tower of the Sun, you ordered the excavation and construction of a special vault. In this magnificent chamber wrought of granite and gold, you placed the seven Lorestones of Nyxator, the gems of Kai power that you had recovered during your quest for the Magnakai. It was here, bathed in the golden light of those radiant gems, that you spent countless hours in pursuit of perfection. Sometimes alone, sometimes in the company of your two able advisors—Banedon and Rimoah—you worked hard to develop your innate Grand Master Disciplines, and grasp the fundamental secrets of Left-Handed and Old Kingdom Magic. During this time you noticed many remarkable changes taking place within your body: you became physically and mentally stronger, your five primary senses sharpened beyond all that you had experienced before, and, perhaps most remarkably, your body began to age at a much slower rate. Now, for every five years that elapse you age but one year.

At this time many changes were occurring beyond the borders of Sommerlund. In the regions to the northeast of Magador and the Maakengorge, the Elder Magi of Dessi and the Herbwardens of Bautar were working together in an effort to restore the dusty volcanic wasteland to its former fertile state. It was the first tentative step towards the reclamation of all the Darklands. However, their progress was painfully slow, and both parties were resigned to the fact that their efforts to undo the damage caused by the Darklords would take not years but centuries to complete.

In the far west, the Drakkarim had retreated to their homelands and were engaged in a bloody war against the Lencians. Much of southern Nyras had been reclaimed by the armies of King Sarnac, the Lencian commander, and his flag now flew over territory which, two thousand years ago, had once been part of Lencia.

Following the destruction of the Darklords of Helgedad, the Giaks, the most prolific in number of all of Gnaag's troops, fled into the Darklands and sought refuge in the gigantic city-fortresses of Nadgazad, Aarnak, Gournen, Akagazad and Kaag. Within each of these hellish strongholds fierce fighting broke out as remnants of the Xaghash (lesser Darklords) and the Nadziranim (evil practitioners of Right-Handed Magic who once aided individual Darklord masters) fought for control. It is widely believed that by the time the Elder Magi and the Herbwardens reach the walls of these strongholds they will encounter no resistance; the occupants will have long since brought about their own extinction. Elsewhere, throughout Northern Magnamund, peace reigns victorious and the peoples of the Free Kingdoms rejoice in the knowledge that the age of the Darklords has finally come to an end. Readily men have exchanged their swords for hoes and their shields for ploughs, and now the only marching they do is along the ruts of their freshly furrowed fields. Few are the watchful eyes that scan the distant horizon in fear of what may appear, although there are still those who maintain their vigilance, for the agents of Naar come in many guises and there are those upon Magnamund who wait quietly in the shadows for the chance to do his evil bidding.

Only a year ago the evil Cener Druids of Ruel attempted to enact Naar's revenge. Secretly, in the laboratories of their foul stronghold of Mogaruith, they had laboured to create a virulent plague virus capable of killing every living creature upon Magnamund, save their own kind. Word of their terrible plan reached Lord Rimoah who immediately urged the rulers of the Freelands to raise armies and invade Ruel. Hurriedly they complied, but the invasion ended in disaster. Seven thousand fighting men entered Ruel intent on storming the fortress of Mogaruith and razing it to the ground. Seven thousand marched into the dark realm; only seventy emerged alive. The Ceners were within days of perfecting their ultimate weapon when you took up the challenge and ventured alone into Mogaruith.

Despite overwhelming odds you thwarted their evil plan by destroying the virus and the means by which it was created.

After emerging from Ruel triumphant, your quest fulfilled, you returned home to Sommerlund and the Kai monastery where you resumed your duties as Grand Master. Three months later, on the day that saw the first fall of winter snow, you were visited by Lord Rimoah. Once again he found himself the reluctant bearer of ill news. Your friend Guildmaster Banedon, whilst helping with the reclamation of wastelands close to the Maakengorge, had been abducted by a war-band of Giaks under the command of Nadziranim sorcerers. A rescue was attempted, but ruthlessly the Nadziranim obliterated those who tried to follow their escape into the Darklands. It was feared that the Nadziranim would try to extract from Banedon the secrets of Left-Handed Magic, so that they

4

might marry it to their own foul sorcery. Such an outcome would have given them extraordinary power, power enough to revive the Darklands. A previous attempt to unite the two paths of Magic had resulted in catastrophe for Sommerlund. In the year MS 5050, Vonotar the Traitor, a magician from the same guild as Banedon, had betrayed his homeland in exchange for the promise of Nadziranim power. It was his act of treachery which brought about the invasion of Sommerlund and the destruction of the First Order of the Kai.

Banedon's survival depended upon a swift rescue from Kaag. Mindful of all that was at stake, courageously you volunteered to enter the city-fortress alone in an attempt to save your friend.

Despite fierce odds you gained entry to Kaag, located Banedon, then snatched him from the foul denizens of that city by way of a daring aerial escape from the upper levels of their great citadel. Banedon was severely weakened by his ordeal at the hands of the Nadziranim and, had it not been for your timely intervention, he would certainly have perished in that grim city-fortress.

The rescue of Guildmaster Banedon and his safe return to Sommerlund was cause for much celebration, especially in the streets and guildhalls of his native city of Toran. For several days you allowed yourself to be feted by the Brotherhood of the Crystal Star before returning to your monastery where, with a feeling of quiet satisfaction, you gladly resumed your duties as Kai Grand Master.

So the year ended and another began, yet even before the snows of winter had begun to thaw, once again your unique skills were being sought in the relentless struggle against Evil. This time the plea for help arrived by way of a foreign ambassador, a special envoy who had travelled thousands of miles from the court of King Sarnac of Lencia. Their war against the Drakkarim, who were under the command of Magnaarn, the High Warlord of Drake, had stagnated ever since the onset of winter and recently the whole campaign had taken a turn for the worse. The Lencians learned that Magnaarn had undertaken a quest for the Doomstone of Darke, an artefact of legendary evil. It was said that this gem was the most powerful of all the Doomstones created by Agarash the Damned during the Age of Eternal Night. Before the demise of the Darklords, this doomstone had rested in the head of the Nyras Sceptre, a magical weapon wielded by Darklord Dakushna, Lord of Kagorst. In the chaos that followed the wake of Dakushna's destruction, the Nyras Sceptre was lost, though many secretly believed it to have been stolen by one of Dakushna's Nadziranim sorcerers. Some months later during the war in Nyras the sceptre reappeared, but the Doomstone was missing from its setting atop the sceptre's platinum haft.

"We fear that Magnaarn is close to finding the Doomstone of Darke," said the Lencian envoy. "Already he possesses the sceptre's haft. My liege, King Sarnac, beseeches you, Grand Master Lone Wolf, to come to our aid. Help us find the Doomstone and thwart Magnaarn's plan, for if he successfully reunites the doomstone and the Nyras sceptre he will command a power capable of our undoing."

"With respect, my lord, surely this one weapon, however evil it may be, is no match when pitted against all the armoured might of Lencia?" you replied diplomatically, as yet unconvinced by the envoy's plea.

"Perhaps so, Grand Master," he replied, "Were the nature of the threat merely the weapon alone. Sadly this is not the only issue here. Until now, the Nadziranim sorcerers who control the strongholds of Kagorst and Akagazad have refused to aid Magnaarn in his war against us. Many times he has begged them for help, for within those fortress walls are thousands of Giaks and other breeds who sought sanctuary there after the defeat of the Darklords. They still possess their weapons and they would make a formidable enemy if ever they were mustered against us.

Magnaarn's possession of the Doomstone of Darke will most certainly influence the Nadziranim. Its power is such that Magnaarn could simply force them to obey his every command. Their refusal would result in their immediate destruction."

Politely you dismissed the envoy whilst you considered your response to his plea. In the solitude of your chamber you pondered the problem, weighing the plight of Lencia against your duties and responsibilities there at the Kai monastery. At length, after careful deliberation, you reached your decision.

6

"Well, my Lord?" enquired the envoy, nervously, upon re-entering your chamber. "Will you help us thwart Magnaarn?"

"Once, not so very long ago, your King and his army aided me during my quest for the Magnakai," you replied. "Perhaps now the time has come for me to repay my debt of gratitude. Yes, I shall help you. I shall return with you to Lencia and champion your cause. I vow that I shall do all in my power to thwart Magnaarn's quest."

THE GAME RULES

You keep a record of your adventure on the *Action Chart* that
you will find in the front of this book. For ease of use, and for
further adventuring, it is recommended that you photocopy these
pages.

For more than five years, ever since the demise of the Darklords
of Helgedad, you have devoted yourself to developing further
your fighting prowess—COMBAT SKILL—and physical stamina—
ENDURANCE. Before you begin this Grand Master adventure you
need to measure how effective your training has been. To do this
take a pencil and, with your eyes closed, point with the blunt end
of it on to the *Random Number Table* on the last page of this
book. If you pick a *O* it counts as zero.

The first number that you pick from the *Random Number Table*
in this way represents your COMBAT SKILL. Add 25 to the number
you picked and write the total in the COMBAT SKILL section of
your *Action Chart* (i.e. if your pencil fell on the number *6* in the
Random Number Table you would write in a COMBAT SKILL of
31). When you fight, your COMBAT SKILL will be pitted against
that of your enemy. A high score in this section is therefore very
desirable.

The second number that you pick from the *Random Number Table*
represents your powers of ENDURANCE. Add 30 to this number
and write the total in the ENDURANCE section of your *Action Chart*
(i.e. if your pencil fell on the number *7* on the *Random Number
Table* you would have 37 ENDURANCE points).

If you are wounded in combat you will lose ENDURANCE points. If at any time your ENDURANCE points fall to zero, you are dead and the adventure is over. Lost ENDURANCE points can be regained during the course of the adventure, but your number of ENDURANCE points can not rise above the number you have when you start an adventure.

If you have successfully completed any of the previous adventures in the Lone Wolf series (Books 1–14), you can carry your current scores of COMBAT SKILL and ENDURANCE points over to Book 15. These scores may include Weapon-mastery, Curing and Psi-surge bonuses obtained upon completion of Lone Wolf Kai (Books 1–5) or Magnakai (Books 6–12) adventures. Only if you have completed these previous adventures will you benefit from the appropriate bonuses in the course of the Grand Master series. You may also carry over any Weapons and Backpack Items you had in your possession at the end of your last adventure, and these should be entered on your new Grand Master _Action Chart_ (you are still limited to two Weapons, but you may now carry up to ten Backpack Items).

However, only the following Special Items may be carried over from the Lone Wolf Kai (1–5) and Magnakai (6–12) series to the Lone Wolf Grand Master series (13-onwards):

CRYSTAL STAR PENDANT	**SOMMERSWERD**
SILVER HELM	**DAGGER OF VASHNA**
JEWELLED MACE	**SILVER BOW OF DUADON**
HELSHEZAG	**KAGONITE CHAINMAIL**

KAI AND MAGNAKAI DISCIPLINES

During your distinguished rise to the rank of Kai Grand Master, you have become proficient in all of the basic Kai and Magnakai Disciplines. These Disciplines have provided you with a formidable arsenal of natural abilities which have served you well in the fight against the agents and champions of Naar, King of the Darkness. A brief summary of your skills is given below:

Weaponmastery

Proficiency with all close combat and missile weapons. Master of unarmed combat; no COMBAT SKILL loss when fighting barehanded.

Animal Control

Communication with most animals; limited control over hostile creatures. Can use woodland animals as guides and can block a non-sentient creature's sense of taste and smell.

Curing

Steady restoration of lost ENDURANCE points (to self and others) as a result of combat wounds. Neutralization of poisons, venoms and toxins. Repair of serious battle wounds.

Invisibility

Mask body heat and scent; hide effectively; mask sounds during movement; minor alterations of physical appearance.

Huntmastery

Effective hunting of food in the wild; increased agility; intensified vision, hearing, smell and night vision.

Pathsmanship

Read languages, decipher symbols, read footprints and tracks. Intuitive knowledge of compass points; detection of enemy ambush up to 500 yards; ability to cross terrain without leaving tracks; converse with sentient creatures; mask self from psychic spells of detection.

Psi-surge
Attack enemies using the powers of the mind; set up disruptive vibrations in objects; confuse enemies.

Psi-screen
Defence against hypnosis, supernatural illusions, charms, hostile telepathy and evil spirits. Ability to divert and re-channel hostile psychic energy.

Nexus
Move small items by projection of mind power; withstand extremes of temperature; extinguish fire by force of will; limited immunity to flames, toxic gases, corrosive liquids.

Divination
Sense imminent danger; detect invisible or hidden enemy; telepathic communication; recognize magic-using and/or magical creatures; detect psychic residues; limited ability to leave body and spirit-walk.

GRAND MASTER DISCIPLINES

Now, through the pursuit of new skills and the further development of your inate Kai abilities, you have set out upon a path of discovery that no other Kai Grand Master has ever attempted with success. Your determination to become the first Kai Supreme Master, by acquiring total proficiency in all twelve of the Grand Master Disciplines, is an awe-inspiring challenge. You will be venturing into the unknown, pushing back the boundaries of human limitation in the pursuit of greatness and the cause of Good. May the blessings of the gods Kai and Ishir go with you as you begin your brave and noble quest.

In the years following the demise of the Darklords you have reached the rank of Kai Grand Defender, which means that you have mastered *four* of the Grand Master Disciplines listed below. It is up to you to choose which four Disciplines these are. As all of the Grand Master Disciplines will be of use to you at some point during your adventure, pick your four skills with care. The correct use of a Grand Master Discipline at the right time could save your life.

SPEAR

DAGGER

MACE

SHORT SWORD

WARHAMMER

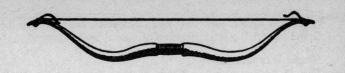

BOW

QUARTERSTAFF

BROADSWORD

AXE

SWORD

When you have chosen your four Disciplines, enter them in the Grand Master Disciplines section of your *Action Chart*.

Grand Weaponmastery

This Discipline enables a Grand Master to become supremely efficient in the use of all weapons. When you enter combat with one of your Grand Master weapons, you add 5 points to your COMBAT SKILL. The rank of Kai Grand Defender, with which you begin the Grand Master series, means you are skilled in *two* of the weapons listed overleaf.

Animal Mastery

Grand Masters have considerable control over hostile, non-sentient creatures. Also, they have the ability to converse with birds and fishes, and use them as guides.

Deliverance (*Advanced Curing*)

Grand Masters are able to use their healing power to repair serious battle wounds. If, whilst in combat, their ENDURANCE is reduced to 8 points or less, they can draw upon their mastery to restore 20 ENDURANCE points. This ability can only be used once every 20 days.

Assimilance (*Advanced Invisibility*)

Grand Masters are able to effect striking changes to their physical appearance, and maintain these changes over a period of a few days. They also have mastered advanced camouflage techniques that make them virtually undetectable in an open landscape.

Grand Huntmastery

Grand Masters are able to see in total darkness, and have greatly heightened senses of touch and taste.

Grand Pathsmanship

Grand Masters are able to resist entrapment by hostile plants, and have a super-awareness of ambush, or the threat of ambush, in woods and dense forests.

Kai-surge

When using their psychic ability to attack an enemy, Grand Masters may add 8 points to their COMBAT SKILL. For every round in which Kai-surge is used, Grand Masters need only deduct 1 ENDURANCE point. Grand Masters have the option of using a weaker form of psychic attack called **Mindblast**. When using this lesser skill, they may add 4 points to their COMBAT SKILL without the loss of any ENDURANCE points. (Kai-surge, Psi-surge, and Mindblast cannot be used simultaneously.)

Grand Masters cannot use Kai-surge if their ENDURANCE score falls to 6 points or below.

Kai-screen
In psychic combat, Grand Masters are able to construct mind fortresses capable of protecting themselves and others. The strength and capacity of these fortresses increases as a Grand Master advances in rank.

Grand Nexus
Grand Masters are able to withstand contact with harmful elements, such as flames and acids, for upwards of an hour in duration. This ability increases as a Grand Master advances in rank.

Telegnosis *(Advanced Divination)*
This Discipline enables a Grand Master to spirit-walk for far greater lengths of time, and with far fewer ill effects. Duration, and the protection of his inanimate body, increases as a Grand Master advances in rank.

Magi-Magic
Under the tutelage of Lord Rimoah, you have been able to master the rudimentary skills of battle magic, as taught to the Vakeros—the native warriors of Dessi. These skills include the use of basic Magi-Magic spells such as *Shield*, *Power Word*, and *Invisible Fist*. As you advance in rank, so will your knowledge and mastery of Old Kingdom Magic increase.

Kai-alchemy
Under the tutelage of Guildmaster Banedon, you have mastered the elementary spells of Left-Handed Magic, as practised by the Brotherhood of the Crystal Star. These spells include *Lightning Hand*, *Levitation*, and *Mind Charm*. As you advance in rank, so will your knowledge and mastery of Left-Handed Magic increase, enabling you to craft new Kai weapons and artefacts.

If you successfully complete the mission as set in Book 15 of the Lone Wolf Grand Master series, you may add a further Grand Master Discipline of your choice to your *Action Chart* in Book 16.

15

For every Grand Master Discipline you possess, in excess of the original four Disciplines you begin with, you may add 1 point to your basic COMBAT SKILL score and 2 points to your basic ENDURANCE points score. These bonus points, together with your extra Grand Master Discipline(s), your original four Grand Master Disciplines and any Special Items that you have found and been able to keep during your adventures, may then be carried over and used in the next Grand Master adventure, which is called *The Legacy of Vashna*.

EQUIPMENT

Before you set off on your long journey to Lencia, you take with you a map of the lands and territories of the Western Tentarias (see the inside front cover of this book) and a pouch of gold. To find out how much gold is in the pouch, pick a number from the *Random Number Table* and add 20 to the number you have picked. The total equals the number of Gold Crowns inside the pouch, and you should now enter this number in the "Gold Crowns" section of your *Action Chart*.

If you have successfully completed any of the previous Lone Wolf adventures (Books 1–14), you may add this sum to the total sum of Crowns you already possess. Fifty Crowns is the maximum you can carry, but additional Crowns can be left in safe-keeping at your monastery.

You can take five items from the list below, again adding to these, if necessary, any you may already possess from previous adventures. (Remember, you are still limited to two Weapons, but you may now carry a maximum of ten Backpack Items.)

SWORD (Weapons)

BOW (Weapons)

QUIVER (Special Items). This contains six arrows; record them on your Weapons List.

16

AXE (Weapons)

4 MEALS (Meals). Each Meal takes up one space in your Backpack.

ROPE (Backpack Item)

POTION OF LAUMSPUR (Backpack Item).
This potion restores 4 ENDURANCE points to your total when swallowed after combat. There is enough for only one dose.

SPEAR (Weapons)

DAGGER (Weapons)
List the five items that you choose on your *Action Chart*, under the appropriate headings, and make a note of any effect they may have on your ENDURANCE points or COMBAT SKILL.

Equipment—How to use it

Weapons
The maximum number of weapons that you can carry is *two*. Weapons aid you in combat. If you have the Grand Master Discipline of Grand Weaponmastery and a correct weapon, it adds 5 points to your COMBAT SKILL. If you find a weapon during your adventure, you may pick it up and use it.

Bows and Arrows

During your adventure there will be opportunities to use a bow and arrow. If you equip yourself with this weapon, and you possess at least one arrow, you may use it when the text of a particular section allows you to do so. The bow is a useful weapon, for it enables you to hit an enemy at a distance. However, a bow cannot be used in hand-to-hand combat, therefore it is strongly recommended that you also equip yourself with a close combat weapon, such as a sword or an axe.

In order to use a bow you must possess a quiver and at least one arrow. Each time the bow is used, erase an arrow from your *Action Chart.* A bow cannot, of course, be used if you exhaust your supply of arrows, but the opportunity may arise during your adventure for you to replenish your stock of arrows.

If you have the Discipline of Grand Weaponmastery with a bow, you may add 3 points to any number that you pick from the *Random Number Table,* when using the bow.

Backpack Items

These must be stored in your Backpack. Because space is limited, you may keep a maximum of ten articles, including Meals, in your Backpack at any one time. You may only carry one Backpack at a time. During your travels you will discover various useful items which you may decide to keep. You may exchange or discard them at any point when you are not involved in combat.

Any item that may be of use, and which can be picked up on your adventure and entered on your *Action Chart* is given either initial capitals (e.g. Gold Dagger, Magic Pendant), or is clearly labelled as a Backpack Item. Unless you are told that it is a Special Item, carry it in your Backpack.

Special Items

Special Items are not carried in the Backpack. When you discover a Special Item, you will be told how or where to carry it. The maximum number of Special Items that can be carried on any adventure is twelve.

Food

Food is carried in your Backpack. Each Meal counts as one item. You will need to eat regularly during your adventure. If you do not have any food when you are instructed to eat a Meal, you will lose 3 ENDURANCE points. However, if you have chosen the Discipline of Grand Huntmastery, you will not need to tick off a Meal when instructed to eat.

Potion of Laumspur

This is a healing potion that can restore 4 ENDURANCE points to your total when swallowed after combat. There is enough for one dose only. If you discover any other potion during the adventure, you will be informed of its effect. All potions are Backpack Items.

RULES FOR COMBAT

There will be occasions during your adventure when you have to fight an enemy. The enemy's COMBAT SKILL and ENDURANCE points are given in the text. Lone Wolf's aim in the combat is to kill the enemy by reducing his ENDURANCE points to zero while losing as few ENDURANCE points as possible himself.

At the start of a combat, enter Lone Wolf's and the enemy's ENDURANCE points in the appropriate boxes on the "Combat Record" section of your *Action Chart*.

The sequence for combat is as follows:

1. Add any extra points gained through your Grand Master Disciplines and Special Items to your current COMBAT SKILL total.

2. Subtract the COMBAT SKILL of your enemy from this total. The result is your Combat Ratio. Enter it on the *Action Chart*.

Example

Lone Wolf (COMBAT SKILL 32) is attacked by a pack of Doomwolves (COMBAT SKILL 30). He is taken by surprise and is not given the opportunity of evading their attack. Lone Wolf has the Grand Master Discipline of Kai-surge to which the Doomwolves are not immune, so Lone Wolf adds 8 points to his COMBAT SKILL, giving him a total COMBAT SKILL of 40.

He subtracts the Doomwolf pack's COMBAT SKILL from his own, giving a *Combat Ratio* of +10. (40 − 30 = +10). +10 is noted on the *Action Chart* as the *Combat Ratio*.

3. When you have your Combat Ratio, pick a number from the *Random Number Table*.

4. Turn to the COMBAT RESULTS TABLE on the inside back cover of this book. Along the top of the chart are shown the Combat Ratio numbers. Find the number that is the same as your Combat Ratio and cross-reference it with the random number that you have picked. (The random numbers appear on the side of the chart.) You now have the number of ENDURANCE points lost by both Lone Wolf and his enemy in this round of combat. (*E* represents points lost by the enemy; *LW* represents points lost by Lone Wolf.)

Example
The Combat Ratio between Lone Wolf and the Doomwolf Pack has been established as +10. If the number taken from the *Random Number Table* is a 2, then the result of the first round of combat is:

Lone Wolf loses 3 ENDURANCE points (plus an additional 1 point for using Kai-surge). This loss is in addition to the loss suffered as a result of combat.
Doomwolf Pack loses 9 ENDURANCE points.

5. On the *Action Chart,* mark the changes in ENDURANCE points to the participants in the combat.

6. Unless otherwise instructed, or unless you have an option to evade, the next round of combat now starts.

7. Repeat the sequence from Stage 3.

This process of combat continues until ENDURANCE points of either the enemy or Lone Wolf are reduced to zero, at which point the one with the zero score is declared dead. If Lone Wolf is dead, the adventure is over. If the enemy is dead, Lone Wolf proceeds but with his ENDURANCE points reduced.

Evasion of combat

During your adventure you may be given the chance to evade combat. If you have already engaged in a round of combat and decide to evade, calculate the combat for that round in the usual manner. All points lost by the enemy as a result of that round are ignored, and you make your escape. Only Lone Wolf may lose ENDURANCE points during that round (but then that is the risk of running away!). You may only evade if the text of the particular section allows you to do so.

GRAND MASTER'S WISDOM

Your mission to thwart Magnaarn's quest for the Doomstone of Darke will be fraught with deadly dangers. Be wary and on your guard at all times, for the warriors of Nyras are still a formidable enemy despite their recent defeats on the battlefields of the Western Tentarias.

Some of the things that you will find during your mission will be of use to you in this and future Lone Wolf books, while others may be red herrings of no real value at all. If you discover items, be selective in what you choose to keep.

Pick your four Grand Master Disciplines with care, for a wise choice will enable any player to complete the quest, no matter how weak their initial COMBAT SKILL and ENDURANCE scores may be. Successful completion of previous Lone Wolf adventures, although an advantage, is not essential for the completion of this Grand Master adventure.

The lives of thousands of Lencian crusaders besieging the city of Darke and, ultimately, the final outcome of their war against the hated Drakkarim depends on the success of your mission. May the light of Kai and Ishir be your guide as you venture into the helotry of Nyras.

For Sommerlund and the Kai!

IMPROVED GRAND MASTER DISCIPLINES

As you rise through the higher levels of Kai Grand Mastery, you will find that your Disciplines will steadily improve. For example, if you possess the Discipline of Grand Nexus when you reach the Grand Master rank of Grand Thane, you will be able to pass freely through Shadow Gates and explore the nether realms of Aon and the Daziarn Plane.

If you are a Grand Master who has reached the rank of Sun Knight, you will now benefit from improvements to the following Grand Master Disciplines:

Grand Weaponmastery
Sun Knights with this discipline are able to wield two-handed weapons (e.g. Broadsword, Quarterstaff, Spear, etc.) with full effect, using only one hand.

Deliverance
Sun Knights who possess this skill are able to repair serious wounds sustained by creatures other than themselves. By the laying of hands upon the affected creature's body, a Sun Knight can cause an open wound (or other serious injury) to mend itself. The speed at which this healing takes place increases as a Grand Master rises in rank.

Grand Pathsmanship
Kai Sun Knights with this skill are able to repel at will all normal-sized insects within a radius of three yards. The range and numbers of insects so affected increases considerably as a Grand Master rises in rank.

Grand Nexus
Sun Knights who possess Mastery of this Discipline are able to feign death. By placing themselves into a state of suspended animation, outwardly they are able to achieve all semblance of being truly dead. However, whilst in this state the only sense that a Sun Knight retains is the ability to hear.

Telegnosis

Sun Knights who possess this Discipline are able to communicate telepathically over great distances. Initially the range of this ability is approximately 100 miles, but this distance increases as a Grand Master rises in rank.

Kai-alchemy

Grand Masters who have reached the rank of Sun Knight are able to use the following Brotherhood spells:

Halt Missile—This causes any projected or hurled missile (i.e. arrows, axes, crossbow bolts, etc.) which may pose an immediate threat to the life of a Sun Knight, to cease its flight and remain stationary in mid-air. The effect of the spell lasts for 2–3 seconds, allowing the Sun Knight sufficient time to move away from its line of flight. Initially only one missile can be affected by this spell, but the number increases as a Grand Master rises in rank.

Strength—By casting this spell, a Sun Knight is able to greatly increase his or her physical strength for a short duration. It can be used to lift or move heavy objects, or to effect a temporary increase in COMBAT SKILL and ENDURANCE scores whilst fighting an enemy in unarmed combat.

The nature of any additional improvements and how they affect your Grand Master Disciplines will be noted in the "Improved Grand Master Disciplines" section of future Lone Wolf books.

LEVELS OF KAI GRAND MASTERSHIP

The following table is a guide to the rank and titles you can achieve at each stage of your journey along the road of Kai Grand Mastership. As you successfully complete each adventure in the Lone Wolf Grand Master series, you will gain an additional Grand Master Discipline and progress towards the pinnacle of Kai perfection—to become a Kai Supreme Master.

No. of Grand Master Disciplines acquired	Grand Master Rank
1	Kai Grand Master Senior
2	Kai Grand Master Superior
3	Kai Grand Sentinel
4	Kai Grand Defender—*You begin the Lone Wolf Grand Master adventures at this level of Mastery*
5	Kai Grand Guardian
6	Sun Knight
7	Sun Lord
8	Sun Thane
9	Grand Thane
10	Grand Crown
11	Sun Prince
12	Kai Supreme Master

1

Having pledged your help, you commence preparations for your long journey to Lencia. You have many things you wish to attend to before you depart and so you invite Lord Floras, the Lencian envoy, to enjoy the hospitality of the monastery for a few days in order that you can settle your most pressing obligations. To your surprise he declines your invitation and insists that you leave at once, for he is anxious to return immediately to his distant homeland. Respectfully he reminds you that time does not favour your quest. By ship and by horse his journey to the monastery took more than a month to complete, and with Magnaarn already so near to finding the Doomstone of Darke, he fears that further delays could prove disastrous.

Mindful of the great distance which needs to be traversed, you hurriedly dispatch a journeyman to Toran. He carries your request for help which is addressed to Lord Rimoah, your most trusted friend and advisor, who is presently attending to Guild-master Banedon in his convalescence. Early next morning Lord Rimoah arrives at the monastery in person, aboard the vessel that is to be the answer to your dilemma: *Skyrider*—Banedon's flying ship.

Warmly you greet your old friend, then you introduce him formally to Lord Floras. The two talk at length about the war in the west, and Rimoah concludes the discussion by voicing his approval of your decision to go to King Sarnac's aid. Then he offers some words of warning.

"Be in no doubt, Grand Master," he says, "This mission you have chosen to fulfil will be as perilous as any you have undertaken in the past. Magnaarn is a cunning adversary and this stone he seeks is possessed of a deadly evil. Do not underestimate your enemy. If he should succeed in his quest then I fear the lands of the Western Tentarias will never be at peace."

Turn to **127**.

2

As you search the smouldering ruins, you discover little has survived the fire which, at its height, must have transformed this town into a blazing inferno. The charred bones and skulls of those who died in the battle are strewn everywhere, and no attempt has been made to bury them. You are examining the remains of a Drakkar sword when suddenly you hear Schera calling you. His voice is full of urgency. You discard the sword and hurry back to the main street to find out what is wrong.

Turn to **167**.

3

You deal the ice a mighty blow and it splits wide open. For a moment you fear you are already too late to save your guide, then suddenly his head bobs out of the icy water and you grab hold of his collar before he disappears once again.

You haul him out of the lake and lay him on the frozen surface. His skin is a deep shade of violet and his entire body is shaking uncontrollably. You know that he is in a serious condition but at least he is still alive. Using your healing skills, you transmit some of your body warmth through your hands to his chest and face and, within a few minutes, he comes out of shock and his body returns to its normal temperature. Your prompt action has saved his life, but it has also drained you of 3 ENDURANCE points.

Adjust your ENDURANCE points score accordingly and then turn to **142**.

4

There is a dull click and the great iron door swings slowly open to reveal a dark chamber constructed entirely of polished black rock. Revealed in the torchlight is a throne of rough-hewn marble, upon which there rests the skeletal remains of a warrior clad in mouldering furs. Bare bone gleams dully through a clinging mass of muscle and sinew, now shrunken to an iron-hard texture, and upon its skull there rests a helm of solid gold. Set into the face of this helm is an emerald as large as your fist.

Prarg approaches the throne, tempted by the magnificent emerald, but he halts the moment you warn him that the helm is protected by a magical trap. You sense that a powerful spell of warding encircles the throne; to touch the crown would activate the spell, thereby unleashing a blast of destructive energy. The thought of being blown to atoms serves to dampen Prarg's curiosity and sheepishly he returns to your side. You give the booby-trapped throne a wide berth and leave the chamber by a smooth-walled tunnel in the far wall. But you have taken no more than a dozen steps when a chill of premonition runs like a trickle of icy cold water down your spine. You halt and reach for your weapon.

Then a loud voice booms out, destroying the silence.

"Welcome, Lone Wolf. Welcome to your tomb!"

Instinctively you know that it is the voice of Warlord Magnaarn.

Turn to **252**.

5

Rising into view at the top of the stairs comes another tunnel stalker, the mate of the one you encountered earlier. Mindful of that combat, you decide to seize the initiative and attack this beast before it reaches the top of the stairs.

Tunnel Stalker:
COMBAT SKILL 38   ENDURANCE 40

Because of the speed of your attack, and the advantage of fighting from higher ground, increase your COMBAT SKILL score by 3 points for the duration of this fight.

If you win this combat, turn to **82**.

6

You raise your weapon and steady yourself as the two Ciquali clamber over the gunwale. For a moment they glare at you with hideous, bulging eyes, their throat sacs swelling and collapsing rapidly as they approach the moment to strike. Then, with a shrill screech, they spring simultaneously towards your chest.

Ciquali: COMBAT SKILL 32   ENDURANCE 28

If you win this combat, turn to **134**.

7

The scout places two fingers to his lips and gives a long, warbling whistle. The sound makes the mercenaries spin around and stare in your direction, and you hear one of them whistle twice in reply. Your scout then asks that you be allowed to enter their camp. There is a long pause, then a heavily-accented voice replies, "Show yourselves."

Relief that you are human, and not Drakkarim, is displayed clearly on the faces of these League-landers when the four of you stand up and walk slowly towards their camp. They offer their apologies for firing on you and one suggests that he escorts you to meet their leader—Baron Maquin. Politely you accept his offer.

Turn to **264**.

8

You focus a ball of psychic energy at the advancing creature and unleash it with unexpected results. The beast possesses phenomenal natural psychic abilities which absorb the shock of your attack, enabling it to shrug off a mental assault which would devastate many creatures twice its size.

Turn to **267**.

9

You search through the many cases and boxes which lie scattered around this cluttered cabin, and you discover the following which may be of use to you during your mission:

Signet Ring
Bow
3 Arrows
Sword
2 potions of Laumspur (each restores 4 ENDURANCE points)
Hourglass
Brass Key
Dagger

If you decide to keep any of the above, remember to make the necessary adjustments to your *Action Chart*.

To continue, turn to **251**.

10

Beyond the portal you discover a narrow flight of stone steps. Quickly you climb these stairs, spurred on by the wintery chill which grows steadily colder as you ascend. You count fifty steps before you eventually arrive at a chamber which is heaped with rubble. Its only door is blocked by debris and huge slabs of marble, making an immediate exit impossible. But it is not the door which commands your attention; it is a narrow circular shaft which is set into the middle of the ceiling. It is the source of the cold, wintery draft.

Expectantly, you step closer and investigate this shaft. For the most part it is dark, but you can see glimmers of grey daylight high above, and you can hear the whistling of the wind. But you can also hear another sound, one that is quite unexpected. It is a buzzing, insectile noise. You focus upon the darkness and suddenly you see that the noise comes from nests of winged insects which are fixed all along the inside of the shaft.

If you possess Grand Pathsmanship, and have reached the rank of Sun Knight, turn to **240**.
If you do not possess this Discipline, or have yet to reach this level of Kai rank, turn to **281**.

11

You step away from the two dead Tukodaks, sheathe your weapon and turn around to find Prarg standing by your side. He thanks you for saving him from the Tukodak's spear and then he helps you to hide the bodies of the two slain guards beneath some undergrowth in the surrounding ruins. Before you leave them, a quick search of their packs and pockets reveals the following items:

Enough food for 1 Meal
Dagger
2 Swords
Bow
4 Arrows

If you wish to take and keep any of the above items, remember to adjust your *Action Chart* accordingly.

To enter the unguarded tower, turn to **199**.

12

As the deadly crossbow bolts scream towards you and the Captain, you open your hand and thrust your palm into Prarg's back, pushing him forward. This swift action saves him from the first bolt, but it robs you of time in which to react to the second. It strikes and red-hot pain flares up your arm as the iron-tipped bolt gouges a deep furrow of flesh from the back of your wrist: lose 4 ENDURANCE points.

The lookouts fumble with their crossbows, desperate to fire again, but before they can reload you have disappeared along the beach. Shortly you reach a small secluded cover where Prarg discovers a rusty anchor. It is a landmark, left on purpose by agents of King Sarnac to point the way to the cave where they have left your boat and provisions. You find the cave and together you haul the boat down the beach and raise its coal-black sail before pushing it out into the icy waters of the Tentarias.

Once aboard, you trim the sail whilst Prarg takes charge of the rudder. There is a good wind and within minutes your tiny craft is bobbing towards the far western channel of the Hellswamp, twenty miles distant. You ask Prarg if this dark estuary has a name, and he replies, "Yes. The Drakkarim call it 'Dakushna's Channel' after the Darklord who once commanded the city-fortress of Kagorst. They say it is a fitting dedication, for the waterway is as deadly and as treacherous as the creature after whom it is named."

Turn to **55**.

13

During your trek through the forest, Prarg tells you a little about the history of this land. You learn that the whole of Nyras was once known as Northern Lencia until it was lost to the invading Drakkarim during the Darkdawn War. Many crusades and campaigns have been launched over the centuries to try and recapture this territory, but none, until now, have been successful. The Drakkarim built a fortress on the ruins of the Lencian capital, which was called Gamir, which they renamed Nagamir after their victory. But later, when the Drakkarim allied themselves to the Darklords of Helgedad, the capital was renamed Darke in their honour.

As dusk approaches, you happen by chance upon a forest trail and immediately your tracking skills tell you that it has only recently been constructed. Hoof prints frozen beneath the snow and several sets of footprints tell you that this trail has been used by more than a dozen riders and armoured foot soldiers within the last week.

If you possess Kai-alchemy, turn to **276**.
If you do not possess this Discipline, turn to **41**.

14

Prarg rushes towards the dying Drakkar and, before he can sound his horn, he deals him a killing blow.

"Quick, Sire," he says, sheathing his sword. "Let us away from here lest this knight is not alone."

You leap over the corpse and run down the corridor following closely on the heels of your companion. Soon you come to a junction where you are forced to choose a direction, left or right. You call upon your Kai skills and immediately you sense a strong presence of evil lurking at the end of the right-hand passage. You focus on the source of this evil and determine that it is the Doomstone. You tell Prarg, and together you advance along the passage until you reach a closed door.

If you possess Grand Huntmastery or Grand Pathsmanship, turn to **193**.

If you possess neither of these Disciplines, turn to **207**.

15

You wait as two Drakkarim on horseback come riding past the cabin, then, as soon as the coast is clear, you leap from the ditch and sprint through a gap in the log wall. The moment you reach the cabin you press yourself flat against its rough timbers and peer cautiously through its grimy window.

The cabin is not empty. Inside, you see a Drakkarim sergeant stretching for a bottle of wine that stands on a high shelf. He takes it down, pulls out the cork and helps himself to a long gulp of the glistening, ruby-red liquid. Behind him you can see the edge of the table; his body is obscuring the map.

If you wish to enter the cabin and attack the soldier while he is distracted, turn to **241**.

If you choose to remain where you are and continue your observations, turn to **115**.

16

With brave determination you begin the laborious task of clearing away the rock and rubble which fills this stairwell. You are fearful that it may take you several days to reach the next level and so it comes as a welcome surprise when, after just a few minutes' work, you see a gap appearing at the top of the mound. A gust of cold, wintery air wafts through this breach, rekindling your hopes of reaching the surface. Revived by the cold clean air, you attack the rubble with renewed vigour. But then your hopes are shaken when you hear a sinister sound; behind you, a tunnel stalker is climbing the stairs to the landing.

If you possess Kai-alchemy, and have reached the rank of Sun Knight or higher, turn to **232**.

If you do not possess this Discipline, or have yet to reach this level of Kai training, turn to **5**.

17

Using your advanced Kai skills you conjure up a cloud of fog which completely obscures you from the sight of the approaching lookouts.

"Hurry, Captain!" you whisper, as you pull Prarg to his feet, "we must get away before the wind destroys our screen."

The lookouts stumble into the fog and you hear them cursing as you make good your escape along the beach. You soon outdistance them and, a few minutes later, you happen upon a small secluded cove where Captain Prarg, to his delight, discovers a rusty anchor. At first you cannot fathom why this should please him so, then he tells you that it is a landmark, left on purpose by agents of King Sarnac to point the way to the cave where they have left your boat and provisions. You find the cave and together you haul the boat down the beach and raise its coal-black sail before pushing it out into the icy waters of the Tentarias.

Once aboard, you trim the sail whilst Prarg takes charge of the rudder. There is a good wind and within minutes your tiny craft is bobbing towards the far western channel of the Hellswamp, twenty miles distant. You ask Prarg if this dark estuary has a name, and he replies, "Yes. The Drakkarim call it 'Dakushna's Channel' after the Darklord who once commanded the city-fortress of Kagorst. They say it is a fitting dedication, for the waterway is as deadly and as treacherous as the being after whom it is named."

Turn to **55**.

18

Towards you stalks a great albino creature as big as a bear. Two huge tusks protrude from its dripping jaws, and it yawns hungrily as slowly it draws closer and closer to you and your companion, attracted by the prospect of easy prey. The beast coughs and advances yet another step, its stubby tail twitching angrily. Prarg panics and he shouts "Run" as it fixes him with its fearsome pink eyes. Then the creature senses his fear and at once it comes bounding toward you with its great jaws agape in readiness to bite.

A great bear-like creature stalks towards you, two huge
tusks protruding from his dripping jaws.

If you have a Bow and wish to use it, turn to **70**.
If you do not have a Bow, or choose not to use it, turn to **196**.

19

With bated breath you watch as the cavalry approaches. You recognize them to be Zagganozod, a unit of armoured Drakkarim cavalry of a type you once encountered many years ago, during a quest that took you to the land of Eru.

The enemy horsemen reach the road where they draw their mounts to a halt. They exchange a few words, then they turn their horses towards Darke and gallop away towards the battle that is raging around its walls. As soon as they are out of earshot, Schera and Maquin's men let out a collective sigh of relief.

Turn to **212**.

20

A barricade has been thrown across the road which leads north out of Shugkona. The Drakkarim posted here have been alerted by the sounds of chaos coming from the square, and hurriedly they are trundling an armoured wagon across a gap at the centre of the barricade to seal off the exit completely. You slap your horse's rump and gallop towards this shrinking gap, but three spear-wielding guards see you approaching and they rush forward to challenge you with their weapons held ready to strike.

If you possess Kai-alchemy, and wish to use it, turn to **298**.
If you possess Kai-surge, and have reached the rank of Kai Grand Guardian or higher, turn to **280**.
If you possess neither of these skills, or have yet to reach the required level of Kai Grand Mastership, turn instead to **259**.

21

Schera wakes you shortly before dawn and wearily you rise from your makeshift bed. Mindful of the journey ahead, you make a brief search of the armoury and discover a few weapons, and other items, which could prove useful:

    6 Arrows
    Quiver
    Dagger
    Sword
    Spear

If you wish to keep any of these items, remember to adjust your *Action Chart* accordingly.

The Captain sends word to his men to find boats for the voyage downstream. The order is duly carried out and, within the hour, twenty small craft have been brought to the icy river on the west side of the stone bridge. Schera appoints ten men to each craft, then you and he step aboard the first boat, cast off, and begin a voyage that will take you towards the coastal city of Darke.

The current is strong and the river is free of obstructions, enabling your flotilla to make swift progress downstream. Much of the river bank is lightly wooded and Schera commands everyone to remain vigilant in case there are Drakkarim among the trees, lying in ambush. You pass through the woods without incident and, shortly before noon, you see the ruined town of Odnenga in the distance. Every building has been raised to the ground and a pall of woodsmoke hangs above the town, fed by fires still smouldering from a battle that took place here several days ago. The river here is blocked by debris and you are forced to put ashore. Schera's men set to work clearing a passage, while you and the Captain scout the ruins in search of information.

A soot-blackened road, running east to west, divides this shattered town into two halves. Schera suggests that you split up and search one half each and you nod in agreement.

    If you wish to search the north side of this ruined town, turn to **2**.
    If you choose to search the south side, turn to **266**.

22

As you land your killing blow, the Mawtaw shrieks an unearthly cry and falls to the ground, shivering and twitching fitfully. Then, with unnerving abruptness, it stiffens and lies still. Prarg immediately awakens from his hypnotic trance and, to your surprise, you discover that he has no memory at all of what has happened in the last hour.

Quickly you hurry away from the carcass of the slain Mawtaw and press on deeper into the forest. Your instinct and pathsmanship skills lead you in a northerly direction and you cover more than five miles before the trees begin to thin out. Then you emerge from the forest to be greeted by a spectacular sight.

Turn to **174.**

23

You are ushered into a lavish chamber that is hung with Lencian flags and decorated with exotic fineries from the far-flung corners of Magnamund. All around, guardsmen stand rigidly to attention, their eyes watchful and unblinking behind their silver visors as you approach the high-backed throne which dominates the centre of the room. There before you sits King Sarnac, his silver-grey hair framing a benign face that is still lean and firm despite advancing years.

"Welcome, Grand Master," he says, as he rises from his throne and offers his hand in friendship. "I prayed that you would come to Lencia, to help in the defeat of the cur, Magnaarn, but I did not imagine that you would arrive so soon. You are most welcome."

Gladly you acknowledge the King's greeting and, after he has commended and dismissed Lord Floras, you adjourn with him to an ante-chamber where he tells you about the mission ahead.

"Latest reports from my spies and scouts in the north say that Magnaarn is presently at his army headquarters in Shugkona. Drakkarim have been seen combing a region of the Tozaz forest fifty miles to the north of his headquarters. We think that this is where he believes he'll find the Doomstone of Darke. There are many ancient temples in this area . . . perhaps one is harbouring that evil gem."

The King pauses for a few moments to take some refreshment. From a jewel-encrusted pitcher, he pours two glasses of wine and proffers one to you before continuing. Gratefully you accept and politely you sip the rare vintage whilst listening to the King's plan of action.

"Grand Master," he says, fixing you with his powerful gaze. "if you are to thwart Magnaarn you must travel to Shugkona and seek him out. He must be killed, or, failing this, the infernal Doomstone must be destroyed before he can use it against us. Secrecy is paramount if your mission is to succeed, therefore no attempt to approach Shugkona directly can be made. The lines of battle are drawn up to within fifty miles of that stronghold and the region is alive with Drakkarim. Yet there is still one means of approach that the enemy will not be guarding. I have made provision for a boat to take you to a place we call 'Bear Rock'. It lies on the River Gourneni and is only thirty miles from Magnaarn's headquarters. However, there is one complication . . . to reach the river you must first enter the Hellswamp."

The thought of venturing into that terrible mire fills you with a cold dread, for the Hellswamp is notoriously perilous. King Sarnac recognizes your apprehension and quickly he tries to assuage your fears.

"I understand your anxiety, Grand Master, but rest assured that you will not be entering alone. One of my finest officers will be your guide throughout this mission. He has scouted this route before and he knows how to avoid its many dangers. Once you reach Bear Rock he will guide you through the forest to Shugkona. There you must find out where Magnaarn is and do whatever is necessary to foil his quest. Once you mission has been accomplished, my officer will bring you through our battle lines and see you safely back here to Vadera."

The King reaches for a cord which hangs from a hole in the domed ceiling. He tugs it and a bell tinkles in a distant part of the citadel.

"Now, Grand Master," he says, turning to face the door of the ante-chamber, "the time has come for me to introduce your guide."

If you took part in the Battle of Cetza in a previous Lone Wolf
adventure, turn to **283**.
If you have not taken part in this battle, turn to **114**.

24

You hurry along this tunnel, passing in your stride many fissures
which have opened up the stone floor and shattered the walls. It
ends at a ruined staircase which leads to a landing where you are
confronted by the corpse of a Drakkarim guard. It is slumped
beside a mound of rubble which is blocking the stairs to the level
above. A quick examination of the dead body reveals that both
arms are broken. Injured and trapped here by the rockfall, it appears that this guard eventually died of thirst.

If you wish to search the body further, turn to **224**.
If you wish to attempt to clear away the rubble that is blocking
   the stairs, turn to **311**.

25

Guided by your instincts, you take the Silver Rod from your
pocket and insert it into the lock. It is a perfect fit. Silently the
lock disengages and the door swings open to reveal two Tukodak
guards, both standing with their backs to you. One feels a draft
and glances over his shoulder, but before he can draw a weapon
or warn his comrade, you leap forward and silence them with two
swift and deadly open-handed blows to the napes of their necks.

Turn to **76**.

26

You crash down upon the unsuspecting lancer and send him tumbling from the saddle. Then you seize control of his startled horse
and take off across the square. With your left hand you unholster
the lance and bring it to bear as you gallop headlong towards the
mass of Drakkarim soldiers who stand between you and the
platform.

Turn to **58**.

27

After several unsuccessful attempts to open this lock, you abandon the door and leave the chamber. You are fearful of what may happen if you stay here any longer and so you retrace your steps to the place where you first emerged from the collapsed passage. You pause here for a few minutes to catch your breath, then you continue along the tunnel until, once more, you find yourself standing at the edge of the chasm. You scan this vast and dismal fissure, hoping to find a way to escape from this grim subterranean prison.

If you possess Kai-alchemy, turn to **305**.
If you do not possess this Discipline, turn to **125**.

28

Uncertainty haunts your thoughts as you race across the desolate no man's land that lies between the inner and outer defences of Shugkona. Soon you catch sight of these outer defences. They comprise a line of man-sized wooden casks filled with earth, behind which there stands a squad of Drakkarim archers. Their bows are loaded and aimed ready to fire.

Quickly you steer your horse away from the road and set off across rough, snowy ground towards a distant line of trenches. Fortunately, the defences at the northern perimeter are much weaker than elsewhere. The trenches are empty, the guards having left them earlier to watch Prarg's execution in the main square. However, the rough terrain soon takes its toll upon your already tired horse. It is near to exhaustion, and as you approach the trenches, you fear he is not strong enough to make the jump.

Pick a number from the *Random Number Table*. If you possess Animal Mastery, add 3 to the number you have picked. If you have reached the Kai rank of Grand Guardian or higher, add 1.

If your total score is now *3* or less, turn to **223**.
If it is *4–7*, turn to **78**.
If it is *8* or higher, turn to **149**.

29

"Quickly, Prarg!" you shout, as the advancing pack spreads out, attempting to surround you. "Stand back-to-back. Whatever you do, don't let them separate us or we're done for!"

The Captain obeys your command and, as the first of the snarling war-dogs comes leaping through the air, you steel yourselves to receive its manic attack.

Wild Akataz Pack:
COMBAT SKILL 38   ENDURANCE 50

These war dogs are especially susceptible to psychic attack. Double all bonuses you would normally receive should you decide to use a psychic attack during this combat.

If you win the combat, turn to **258**.

30

The slime-smeared steps are narrow and steep and seem to go on forever. You ascend, settling into a steady climbing rhythm, and after a long while you come to a rot-infested door on which your fumbling fingers discover a corroded metal latch. It opens into a dim and lofty chamber, vaulted by massive pillars of marble which are slick with moisture. The ground is carpeted with mottled green fungi, some specimens standing even taller than yourself, and the humid air is thick with spores.

Slowly you make your way across the chamber to an archway which is flanked by stone pillars, carved to resemble two huge open books. Around the base of these book-like pillars you notice several clumps of fleshy fungi which you recognize at once. They are called floroa and are very nutritious. Eagerly you pick and swallow a handful of these floroa—restore 3 ENDURANCE points—before leaving this chamber. (If you wish to take some of this fungi with you, record it on your *Action Chart* as a Back-

pack Item. Consuming this at a later time will restore 3 ENDUR-
ANCE points.)

To continue, turn to **299**.

31

The sight of Prarg being held hostage by these ruthless Drakkarim
fills you with frustrated anger, but you dare not show it. The
slightest provocation could result in the Captain's death. Instead,
you call upon Warlord Magnaarn to show himself; you do not
have to wait long for his response.

Turn to **181**.

32

You slay the Death Knights and bundle their bodies down the
stairs to delay the other Drakkarim. Then, with fear running cold
in your veins, you hurry across to a window on the far side of
the tower. Outside, directly below, you see a Drakkar lancer sitting astride a warhorse. His lance is sheathed in a tubelike scabbard fixed to the rear of his saddle and in his hand he holds aloft
a heavy-bladed cavalry sabre. He is cheering those who are entering the tower and he is completely unaware that you are barely
a few yards away.

Swiftly you climb on to the window ledge, draw your weapon,
then leap on to the unwary lancer below.

Pick a number from the *Random Number Table*. If you possess
Grand Huntmastery, add 3 to the number you have picked.

If your total score is now *4* or less, turn to **139**.
If your total score is now *5* or more, turn to **26**.

33

You follow Prarg to the top of the steps and, as you race along
the body-strewn battlements, you see the fighting which is raging
both inside and outside the city. The battlements end at a tower
where a flight of spiral steps ascend to a circular landing. Here

you wait in the shadows until a troop of Drakkarim pass by. While you are waiting for them to disappear, you look out of the tower through an arrow slit and see the waters of the Gulf of Lencia, and the conflict that is raging across the coastal plain.

"The King's Crusaders breached the city gate three days ago," whispers Prarg. "They were close to taking the city when Magnaarn and his armies arrived. His new-found power shattered the Crusaders, but even though they were broken by it, not all were ejected from the city. Those you saw fighting at the keep are trying to hold on until our allies arrive from Kasland. The fleet is expected at any time. Magnaarn must be slain. He and the sceptre have become one entity—he is now a puppet of a far greater evil."

A shudder runs down your spine as, for the first time since you entered Darke, you feel the presence of the Doomstone. Fear returns to haunt you, the fear that the evil gem will sap your strength, as it did when first you encountered it at the Temple of Antah. If this is still so then Magnaarn may prove impossible to defeat.

Prarg senses your anxiety and he offers some words of advice and hope: "The taking of Darke has weakened the Warlord—he's paid a terrible price. He has been forced to retire from the battle in order to recover his strength and he is presently at his weakest. Now, Sire, is the time to strike."

Beyond the landing lies a corridor which leads to a junction where another passageway crosses from left to right. You look to the right and see that the way is blocked by a heavy steel door. Prarg utters a curse under his breath, then he explains his anger.

"That way leads directly to the Palace Tower. Magnaarn is hiding there, in its uppermost chamber."

Anxiously he glances along the opposite passage and furrows his brow. "Perhaps we can get there by another route," he muses.

If you wish to investigate the closed door, turn to **198**.
If you choose to look for another way of reaching the Palace Tower, turn to **165**.

34

Suddenly you sense that Prarg is walking directly towards a patch of thin ice. You shout a warning but it is already too late. A loud "crack" echoes across the lake as the surface shatters and, in a terrible moment, your companion disappears feet-first into a seething pool of icy grey water.

If you possess a Rope, turn to **190**.
If you do not, turn to **310**.

35

You let fly your arrow and send it deep into the creature's throat. For a few moments the Ciquali looks at you as if unaffected by the arrow, then its eyes roll backwards in their sockets and stiffly it falls backwards over the gunwale to sink without trace beneath the slimy water.

As one, the remaining Ciquali flee from the boat and disappear as quickly as they had come, slipping back to the cold, dark safety of their hiding places beneath the surface. Silence returns, and for a long moment you stand alert, suspecting trickery, then slowly you relax; they have gone.

Aided by your healing skills, Prarg makes a speedy recovery from the battering he sustained in combat with the Ciquali chieftain. The boat, too, has survived the attack and you are able to continue without further delay. As soon as you pass the obstruction, you hoist the sail and catch the prevailing wind which propels you northwards along the channel beyond.

You are hungry after your encounter. Unless you possess Grand Huntmastery, you must now eat a Meal or lose 3 ENDURANCE points.

To continue, turn to **98**.

36

The fight for control of Konozod is swift and bloody. Within the hour the town is under Lencian control, its Drakkarim garrison having been put mercilessly to the sword. However, not all of the enemy perish in the battle. To Captain Schera's dismay, several manage to escape across the river and flee to the west on horseback. He is anxious that they may return with reinforcements to retake the town.

A food store is discovered and, whilst the starving Lencians satiate their hunger, you talk with Captain Schera about the events of the last few weeks which have led to this meeting. Your learn from him that after you were interred in the Temple of Antah, Warlord Magnaarn waged a major offensive against the Lencian army. Having reunited the Doomstone with the Nyras Sceptre, he has, as King Sarnac feared, forced the Nadziranim sorcerers of Kagorst and Akagazad to help him. Their combined skills have wrought great destruction. They attacked and drove through the Lencian lines like demons in an offensive which was swift and deadly. A week ago, Captain Schera and his regiment were cut off and captured in the fighting around Hokidat, after which they were marched here and imprisoned. He considers himself lucky to be alive, for the Drakkarim rarely take prisoners. Then you ask what news he has heard about the war since he came here.

"There's much confusion," he says, wearily. "I've heard talk that most of the mercenaries in Sarnac's pay have deserted us. Some have even joined the enemy. The Drakkarim taunted us, saying that our army had been smashed. They said the remnants have been pushed into the Tentarias, but I dismissed this as lies. One thing is sure, though: Magnaarn intends to raise the seige of Darke. It has become his battle call—'On to Darke?' This cry was on the lips of his troops during the battle at Hokidat. I saw him during this battle. He was leading his army personally, and he was wielding his accursed sceptre, dealing death to all who tried to stand in his way. He possesses a great and terrible power, and I fear that we may now be unable to put an end to his evil ambitions."

If you wish to ask Schera if he knows anything about Captain Prarg, turn to **88.**
If you do not, turn to **214.**

37

On the final tap you hear a faint click, then the door creaks slowly open to reveal a dark and desolate chamber, its brick walls dripping with evil-smelling grey slime.

If you possess Grand Huntmastery, turn to **177**.
If you do not possess this Discipline, turn to **117**.

38

Shortly after midnight you are awoken by the sound of wolves howling. Within a few moments you are on your feet, your weapon in hand as you race up the bank towards the place where you stationed your timberwolf guards. As you crest the bank you see them pacing back and forth, their eyes fixed on the forest's edge, their thick white fur standing on end with anxiety and fear. You scour the treeline and at once you see the cause of their concern: Akataz. A dozen of the leathery black war-dogs are slinking in the shadows, waiting for the chance to attack. These ferocious wild dogs are often used by the Drakkarim and you have encountered them before on several occasions. Mindful of past experiences, you recall a weakness of the breed: they are particularly susceptible to psychic attacks.

Armed with this knowledge, you focus your Magnakai skill of psi-surge upon the pack and launch a sharp blast of psychic energy in their direction. The effect is immediate: the Akataz are traumatized by this sudden assault. Shrieking with fright, the dogs flee from the bank and seek refuge in the dark safety of the Tozaz Forest. Confident that they will not be back, affectionately you pat your two loyal guards then return to the boat to resume your night's rest.

Turn to **194**.

39

The Nadziranim sorcerer has taken on the visage of a great snuffling beast which creeps towards you on six long-clawed feet. A vile, bulbous head is perched uneasily on its immense shoulders and its baleful, milky-coloured eyes roll like balls of mist within

The Nadziranim sorcerer, taking on the visage of a great
sniffling beast, creeps towards you.

its scabrous head. The reeking fur of its body seems to bristle as slowly, with ponderous steps, it draws closer and closer.

If you possess the Sommerswerd, turn to **245**.
If you do not possess this Special Item, turn to **122**.

40

A few moments after the wall closes there is a sound like distant thunder. Then a shudder runs through the floor and clumps of dirt begin to fall from cracks in the ceiling. Your strength is returning, but before you can attempt to escape, there is an almighty explosion and a deluge of rock and damp earth cascades into the passageway. The ceiling and floor are being pulled in opposing directions and, with a grating cry of tortured stone, the heavy portcullis shatters in two. Quickly you crawl beneath a broken section which lies at an angle to the wall, and take cover as countless tons of rock and earth rain down from above.

When at last the destruction ceases you find yourself trapped in the narrow triangular space between the broken portcullis and the wall. Your quick thinking has saved you from physical injury, but, as far as you can tell, you are now buried in a collapsed level of the temple, hundreds of feet below the surface. Confident in the knowledge that, at worse, your stamina and Kai skills alone can keep you alive for several days, you begin the slow and laborious task of digging your way out of this subterranean tomb.

Turn to **141**.

41

Guided by your intuition, you set off with Prarg along the forest trail heading west and soon your tracking skills warn you that you are nearing an enemy encampment. You signal your discovery to Prarg and he follows as stealthily you enter the undergrowth and slip past a line of Drakkarim sentries. From the cover of the dense forest bracken you observe their camp. You count more than two dozen soldiers, plus horses, wagons and shelters. Prarg points to the emblem which adorns all of their uniforms and equipment: a black eagle clutching two fiery swords.

"These are the Tukodak—Warlord Magnaarn's personal guards," he says in a hushed whisper. "We would be wise to avoid them."

You nod in agreement then together you slip away from the camp and head north through the trees.

You are drawn in this direction by something your senses have detected. It is a strong aura of energy, an evil energy which you feel sure must be radiating from the Doomstone of Darke. Within a few minutes you stumble upon a clearing where stands the majestic ruins of an ancient temple. At once you know that this is the Temple of Antah and you sense that the Doomstone is here, lying somewhere deep within the ruins.

Turn to **91**.

42

Stoically, you begin the difficult trek westwards through this dense timberland, following the tracks left behind by Magnaarn's troops. At dusk you reach the forest's edge and stare out across an open expanse of bare, snow-covered plain. There is no cover to be had here, but at least the approaching darkness will help keep you hidden from hostile eyes.

As you emerge from the trees, by chance you notice something half-buried in the undergrowth. A closer look reveals it to be a large Drakkarim backpack. You flip open the buckles to search it and discover it contains the following items:

Bow
2 Arrows
Enough food for 2 Meals
Potion of Alether (increases COMBAT SKILL by 2 points for duration of one combat only)
Bottle of Wine
Bowstring

If you wish to keep any of these items, remember to adjust your *Action Chart* accordingly.

To continue your trek, turn to **94**.

43

You share your premonition of danger with Captain Prarg and wisely he heeds your warning. He suggests you draw in the sail to prevent the wind from propelling your boat towards the raft of weeds, yet once the sail is gathered, still you find yourselves drifting ever nearer to the obstruction.

With weapons drawn, you wait in tense expectation as the boat grazes the edge of the weed-raft. For a few seconds there is an unnatural silence, then suddenly a gurgling screech rends the frosty air. Like sorcery-conjured demons, a dozen ghoulish creatures rise up from the murky depths of the swamp amid a seething froth of bubbles. Swiftly they climb from beneath the weed-raft and slink from other hiding places among the dank thickets of the adjoining bank. Within seconds they have you surrounded.

"Ciquali!" cries Prarg, naming these ghoulish foes. He steps forward, brandishing his sword, and lashes out at the boldest of the dome-headed creatures as it tries to slip aboard. His razor-sharp blade severs its forearm at the wrist, sending a scaly webbed hand spinning into the swamp, trailing green ichor. The beast screams as it falls over the side, yet no sooner has it vanished beneath the surface when two more of its kin grab the gunwales and attempt to haul themselves into the boat.

If you have a Bow and wish to use it, turn to **164**.
If you do not, or choose not to use it, turn to **6**.

44

Your advanced pathsmanship skills locate the faint outline of tracks in the dust which covers the rough stone floor. These tracks were made by a creature that is bigger than yourself, a large-footed biped with clawed toes and an awkward shuffling gait. You are tracing the outline of one footprint with your index finger when suddenly your acute senses warn you that something hostile is approaching along the corridor.

If you wish to avoid a confrontation, you can turn around and hurry along this tunnel in the opposite direction, by turning to **228**.
If you choose instead to draw your weapon and advance to meet this unknown threat, turn to **113**.

45

You crash down upon the unsuspecting lancer, but the shock of impact does not unseat him and desperately he struggles to fend you off. He gouges your cheek with his studded gauntlets before you succeed in knocking him out of the saddle: lose 2 ENDURANCE points.

The lancer falls heavily to the ground, striking his head. Before he can recover his senses, you seize control of the horse and take off across the square. With your left hand you unholster the lance and bring it to bear as you gallop headlong towards the backs of the Drakkarim soldiers who stand between you and the platform.

Turn to **58**.

46

A ragged line of Lencian prisoners are crossing the stone bridge, escorted by a dozen Drakkarim armed with crossbows and spears. The main gates swing open to admit them, and, as the Lencians file through with their heads bowed in defeat, you see that the central square of this town has been turned into a large prisoner-of-war compound. It is enclosed by a crude fence of wire and sharpened stakes, which is patrolled by sentries and Akataz wardogs. From what little you can see you estimate at least two hundred Lencians are being held captive here.

The conditions are shocking. The men are being kept out in the open, without shelter or heat of any kind, and, judging by the state of those already here, it looks as if the Drakkarim are purposefully starving them to death.

Your shock soon turns to anger and you vow to do something to help these prisoners. But before you can think through a plan of action, your Kai senses warn you of approaching footsteps. Two of the Drakkarin escort have slipped away from the line and they are now walking briskly towards the alleyway. One has a large canvas sack slung over his shoulder and, as they draw closer, you are forced to take cover in a shadowy doorway to avoid being seen.

Pick a number from the *Random Number Table*. If you possess Assimilance, add 3 to your score.

If your total score is now *4* or less, turn to **107**.
If it is *5* or more, turn to **235**.

47

Cautiously you descend the slippery hill track and make your approach to the bridge. The thick snow muffles your steps and you are able to reach the cabin without alerting its occupants. You motion to Prarg to take hold of the horse and keep lookout whilst you investigate the stables. Silently you slip alongside the cabin and pass beneath its solitary window.

If you wish to peek through the window, turn to **239**.
If you choose to ignore the window and make your way directly to the stables, turn to **106**.

48

The Drakkar shudders as you land your killing blow. With an open-mouthed look of surprise, he clasps his chest then drops lifelessly to the floor. Quickly you step over his corpse and hurry to the table to study the map. To your disappointment, the map turns out to be merely a construction plan of the encampment. It offers no clues to Magnaarn's present location.

If you wish to search the cabin more thoroughly, turn to **192**.
If you choose to leave the cabin and return to Prarg, turn to **251**.

49

The ambush is swift and devastating, yet despite having been caught completely unawares, the Drakkarim cavalry put up a spirited fight. Their leader is a formidable swordsman and more than a dozen Lencians die beneath his swishing blade before he finds himself in face-to-face combat with a Kai Grand Master.

Zagganozod Captain:
COMBAT SKILL 34   ENDURANCE 36

If you win this combat, turn to **306**.

50

Your super-keen senses warn you that Prarg is walking towards a patch of thin ice. At once you shout a warning and he halts in his tracks. Then, carefully, he retraces his steps and follows in your footsteps as you make a wide detour around this perilous section. An hour later you reach the far side of the lake and hurry into the forest beyond.

Turn to **170**.

51

You take a Gold Crown from your money pouch, flick it in the air, then catch it on the back of your hand. With your advanced skills it is easy for you to sense immediately that the coin is showing heads, but Prarg is not so gifted.

"Heads or tails?" you ask your companion.

Thoughtfully he scratches his chin as he considers his answer.

Pick a number from the *Random Number Table*.

If the number you have picked is *0–4*, turn to **108**.
If it is *5–9*, turn to **268**.

52

Despite your realistic disguise and plausible story, the Tukodak guards are not deceived.

"Gazim!" shouts the spear-wielder, and you are forced to knock Prarg aside to save his life as the angry Drakkar thrusts at his chest. You move back a few paces and draw your weapon just in time to defend yourself as the guards rush to attack.

Tukodaks:
COMBAT SKILL 36   ENDURANCE 32

If you win this combat, turn to **11**.

53

You crash down upon a stack of ale barrels which, in turn, topple and fall, pinning you beneath them. Yet despite your heavy landing, your cat-like reflexes save you from sustaining any serious injuries: lose only 1 ENDURANCE point.

At once you try to extricate yourself from beneath the heavy casks, but a sudden sound causes you to stop and stare at the broken trapdoor. In the alleyway above, you hear the sounds of a struggle taking place: the Drakkarim have found your companion, Prarg, and they are attempting to overpower him by force.

Turn to **203**.

54

The open doors to the tower appear to offer the only means of access to the temple. Because of this, you decide that you will try and overpower the two Tukodak who are standing guard there. Armed with your formidable Kai skills, and with dusk fast turning to darkness, you are confident you will succeed.

You tell Prarg, who is unarmed, to wait here at the forest's edge until you signal for him to join you. Then you stalk towards the tower, your approach masked by your camouflage skills. At first the way is easy, but the last twenty yards of ground to the stone ramp have been cleared of temple debris and this area is completely open, devoid of any cover.

Pick a number from the *Random Number Table*. If you have reached the rank of Kai Grand Guardian, add 1. If you have reached the rank of Sun Knight (or higher) add 2.

If your total score is now 5 or less, turn to **243**.
If it is 6 or higher, turn to **137**.

55

Dawn breaks as you sail into the estuary of Dakushna's Channel. Prarg keeps the boat in the centre of the wide waterway, where the slimy water is deepest and the ever-present risk of grounding upon submerged debris is less likely to befall you.

Soon you are enveloped by the chaotic wilderness of the Hell-swamp and you feel your spirits drop, as if they are being leeched by some unseen vampire. The monotonous view of slime-laden mudflats extends seemingly forever on every side, broken only occasionally by a dead, vine-strangled tree. You both take some comfort in the fact that there is a wind and it is blowing in a favourable direction. Despite the depressing scenery you make good progress until, late in the afternoon, you are forced to lower your sail when you reach a point where unexpectedly the channel splits in two. Prarg says that this split must have occurred recently, for it was not present the last time he sailed this way. Reluctantly he admits that he is not sure which way to go.

Upon the edge of the left bank, in the middle distance, you see a circle of mud huts perched close to the channel's edge. You magnify your vision, but you are unable to discern any signs of life.

Rather than run the risk of approaching this Hellswamp settlement, you decide to take the right-hand channel.

Turn to **213**.

56

"I'll prepare a diversion. When the guards and their dogs are drawn away from the perimeter fence, you must act quickly. You and your men must storm the gates. Once you are free, make your way to the armoury with all haste. You'll find your weapons there."

"That's all very well," replies the Captain, sceptically, "but how do you propose we get into the armoury? It's the most secure building in the town."

"Don't worry about that," you say, with confidence. "I shall be inside, waiting to let you in."

For a few moments the Captain considers your plan in silence. Then, with a nod, he finally agrees.

"Very well, so be it. I'll pass the word."

You watch as he returns to his men, then you leave the fence and retrace your steps to the darkened alleyway.

Turn to **274**.

57

As you charge towards the sentries, they huddle together and set the butts of their wavering spears into the ground in readiness to receive your attack. But a sharp burst of Psi-surge unsettles them and they scatter moments before you come galloping upon them. In the next instant you are through the gap in the barricade and racing along the road beyond. You have passed successfully through the inner defensive line, but, as Prarg quickly points out, you have yet to reach the outer defences of Shugkona.

Turn to **28**.

58

You steer the horse towards the platform and the troops scatter before you. All, that is, save one. He is a Death Knight sergeant, an elite Drakkarim warrior. He curses his comrades for their cowardice and, as you bear down on him with your lance levelled at his chest, he draws his sword and gets ready to meet your attack head-on. Then the tip of your lance strikes his steel breastplace and you are forced back in your saddle with a jolt that leaves you breathless.

Pick a number from the *Random Number Table*. If your current ENDURANCE points score is 12 or higher, add 2 to the number you have picked.

If your total score is now *2* or less, turn to **75**.
If it is *3* or higher, turn to **312**.

59

Your hopes of finding a clear route out of here are soon dashed when you arrive at a ruined staircase. It leads to a landing where you are confronted by the corpse of a Drakkarim guard, slumped beside a mound of rubble which is blocking the stairs to the level above. A quick examination of the dead body reveals that both arms are broken. Injured and trapped here by the falling rocks, it appears that this guard eventually died of thirst.

If you wish to search the body further, turn to **224**.
If you wish to attempt to clear away the rubble that is blocking the stairs, turn to **311**.

60

Prarg has reservations about your decision; he fears that your curiosity could be leading you both straight into the arms of the enemy. You understand his anxiety but you stand by your decision. Time is running against you and some risks must be taken if you are to discover quickly the location of Magnaarn and the Doomstone. With a nod of his head Prarg accepts the logic of your argument, then, as if to reaffirm his loyalty, he draws his sword and offers to lead the way.

Cautiously you follow him through the dense trees, your nerves as taught as bowstrings. As you draw closer, you are able to make out the sounds of wood being chopped, gruff voices and the jingle of horse bridles. Your suspicions are confirmed when you reach the edge of a clearing and see a Drakkarim encampment in the centre of recently-cleared ground. Three log cabins, two only partially completed, stand in the middle of a circular ditch which is backed in turn by a chest-high wall of sharpened stakes. You count more than a hundred Drakkarim labouring to complete this forest outpost, while another fifty or so stand guard along its perimeter wall. They look well-equipped; all are clad in thick furs and studded leather armour, and they wield weapons which are unmistakably fresh from the forge.

Slowly you edge your way around the clearing until you are on the north side of the encampment. Here the perimeter wall has yet to be completed, affording you an unobstructed view of the cabins. You settle yourself behind a fallen tree and patiently you observe the main hut. Suddenly the door swings open and a Drakkarim officer strides out into the snow. He pulls on his iron helm and draws his wolfskin cloak close about him as he goes off to inspect his men's work. The door swings shut, but before it closes, you catch a glimpse of something that sparks your curiosity anew.

Turn to **295**.

61

The moment you strike your killing blow, the creature explodes with a flash of brilliant white light. As the glare fades, you see that nothing whatsoever remains of either its body or spirit. Magnaarn witnesses the death of his servant with a look of pure terror. He screams, and in a moment of panic, he touches the head of the Nyras Sceptre to the floor. There is a tremendous boom, and the floor shudders violently as it is torn wide open by a massive quake.

Hurriedly, Magnaarn makes his escape through a curtained archway. Determined not to allow him to escape, you get ready to leap across the fissure which has opened up the chamber floor. It is no less than twenty feet wide at its narrowest point.

Pick a number from the *Random Number Table*. If you possess the Discipline of Grand Huntmastery and have reached the rank of Kai Grand Guardian or higher, add 2 to the number you have picked.

   If it is *0–6*, turn to **69**.
   If it is *7* or more, turn to **163**.

62

The guard's eyes, made unnaturally large by the lens, narrow as he stares intently across the snowy eastern approaches to the tower. Immediately you slow yourself to a halt, fall to the ground, then begin utilizing your camouflage skills to keep you hidden from his unblinking gaze.

With your cheek pressed flat to the snow, you glance firstly at the guard's face at the observation slit, then to Captain Prarg who is now climbing the stairs to the tower door, his sword ready to hand. He reaches the door, throws it open, and disappears quickly inside. For a few moments there is complete silence, then he reappears, sheathes his bloodied blade, and beckons you to hurry to the tower.

   Turn to **103**.

63

You take some bread and dried meat from your backpack and offer it to your companion. Gratefully he accepts the food and settles himself at the base of a tree where hungrily he consumes every scrap. (Remember to deduct this Meal from your *Action Chart*.)

Meanwhile, you scan the surrounding forest, ever watchful for enemies. For the last hour you have had a growing suspicion that something has been watching you. Your senses detect the presence of a hostile entity, closing from the east. Now the suspicion has become a firm belief, and the moment Prarg finishes his meal, you suggest that you be on your way as swiftly as possible.

Turn to **13**.

64

Reluctantly you abandon your attempt to open this iron portal and turn instead to a sloping passageway which descends to a deeper subterranean level of this ancient temple. You set off down this damp passage and at length it ends at a vault where the only exit appears to be a vertical pit at its centre. Cautiously you approach the pit and peer through its barred grill.

To your surprise, you see the floor of another torchlit passageway less than a dozen feet directly below the grill. With Prarg's help you pull open the rusty cover, then you lower yourself through the hole and drop down into the corridor below, followed by your companion. The pervading aura of evil is stronger now and you feel certain that with every step you are drawing closer to finding the Doomstone. You are thinking to yourself that perhaps your progress has been almost too easy when suddenly you sense imminent danger.

Pick a number from the *Random Number Table*. If you possess Grand Pathsmanship, add 2 to the number you have picked.

If it is *0–6*, turn to **186**.
If it is *7* or higher, turn to **83**.

65

Patiently you keep watch to the north, expecting to see the appearance of enemy cavalry at any moment. You do not have to wait too long, for within minutes of deciphering the crow's warning, you see the first few outriders of a Drakkarim platoon crest the horizon. You magnify your vision and recognize them to be part of Magnaarn's own army. They are carrying lances topped with pennants that bear Magnaarn's personal emblem: an eagle clasping two fiery swords. Steadily these cavalry scouts draw closer. They are riding directly towards the river.

Pick a number from the *Random Number Table*.

If the number you have chosen is *0–6*, turn to **19**.
If it is *7–9*, turn to **242**.

66

As the beast keels over backwards and splashes into the mire, you roll Prarg on to his back then watch as the remaining Ciquali, now leaderless, turn away and disappear as quickly as they had come, slipping back to the cold, dark safety of their hiding places beneath the surface. Silence returns, and for a long moment you stay alert, suspecting trickery, then slowly you relax; they have gone.

Aided by your healing skills, Prarg makes a speedy recovery from the battering he sustained in combat with the Ciquali chieftain. The boat, too, has survived the attack and you are able to continue without further delay. As soon as you pass the obstruction, you hoist the sail and catch the prevailing wind which propels you northwards along the channel beyond.

You are hungry after your encounter. Unless you possess Grand Huntmastery, you must now eat a Meal or lose 3 ENDURANCE points.

To continue, turn to **98**.

67

You make swift progress, helped by the river's strong current. Gradually, as the day unfolds, the surrounding landscape changes from open plain to an expanse of low, rolling hills which are blackened and scarred by war. Ruined hovels smoulder on the horizon and scores of snow-covered corpses, human and otherwise, lie scattered across the fields, their limbs frozen into impossible shapes.

It is late afternoon when you catch sight of a town on the horizon. You check your map and discover it to be Konozod, a fortified Drakkarim stronghold. As the river carries you closer, you magnify your vision and see that it is built upon the left bank of the Shug. A huge stone bridge spans the river, and beneath this you see that the waterway is blocked by a barrier of chained logs.

If you wish to allow your boat to drift towards this barrier, turn to **282**.

If you decide to avoid the barrier, you can put ashore and continue on foot by turning to **209**.

68

The guard's eyes, made unnaturally large by his magical lens, stare out across the snowy eastern approaches to the town. You are in plain view, less than a few dozen yards from his position, yet he fails to notice you racing to join your companion. Shielded by your Kai skills and aided by your fleetness of foot, you reach Prarg unobserved by this watchful defender.

Prarg points ahead, to an alleyway that lies sandwiched between two burnt-out hovels close by the watchtower. You nod to confirm you understand his intentions, and without a word having been spoken, you follow as he runs towards the alley's shadowy entrance.

Turn to **162**.

69

You leap across the gap, but, as you land, you slip on the broken flooring and gash both your knees: lose 2 ENDURANCE points. Cursing your luck, you hobble towards the curtain through which Magnaarn disappeared and pull it aside to find a short flight of stone steps. You climb them and discover that they emerge at a

Magnaarn cowers with his crooked back pressed against
the frost-covered wall.

turret at the very top of the Palace Tower, the highest point in
the city of Darke.

Here you find Magnaarn, cowering with his crooked back pressed
hard against the frost-covered wall. You sense that he has very
nearly succumbed to the evil power of the Doomstone; he is treading a fine line between life and undeath. Yet, even though he is
but a whisker away from eternal damnation, he musters enough
spite to challenge you to a fight to the death.

"Very well, Drakkar," you reply, "Let battle commence."

> Warlord Magnaarn (*with Nyras Sceptre*):
> COMBAT SKILL 48   ENDURANCE 36

If you win this combat, turn to **314**.

70

Swiftly you draw an arrow, take aim, and fire as the beast comes
leaping through the air towards your chest. The arrow thuds into
its furry belly but the momentum of its leap still carries it
forwards.

Pick a number from the *Random Number Table*.

If the number you have picked is *0–4*, turn to **158**.
If it is *5–9*, turn to **234**.

71

Upon reaching the base of the chasm you discover the ground to
be slick with black, foul-smelling mud. It is peppered with broken
slabs of rock, veined marble and other temple debris which have
fallen from the many sundered levels above. You wade through
this ankle-deep slime, following the course of the river as it rushes
towards the brick-lined tunnel at a frightful speed. When you
reach the tunnel entrance, to your relief you discover a solid stone
walkway which runs parallel to the roaring water. From the roof
of this echoing tunnel hang vast, bloated domes of stinking fungi
which give off a grey-green radiance. It is an unwelcoming light,
an illumination born of decay.

You have taken a few hundred paces along the stone walkway when you are confronted by a massive iron grill. It stretches across the entire width of the tunnel and prevents you from continuing further in this direction. Nearby, a heavy chain hangs from a hole in the arched ceiling. Upon closer investigation you discover that it operates a concealed winch which raises and lowers the grill, like the portcullis of a castle. You are about to haul the chain and raise the grill when suddenly you hear a beast-like roar echoing along the tunnel, louder than the rushing water. You sense danger; something is approaching. You release the chain and spin around, your hand reaching instinctively to your weapon, but you are frozen immobile by the terrible sight of the creature that is now moving along the walkway towards you.

If you possess Animal Mastery, turn to **93**.
If you do not possess this Discipline, turn to **286**.

This quarter of the town is now teeming with enemy soldiers, and as you hurry away from the cell window, you know that you are in grave danger of being caught unless you can find somewhere safe to hide.

At length you discover a refuge on the far side of the main square. It is an empty grain storage tower which overlooks Magnaarn's headquarters and the gaol, and it is here that you spend a sleepless night contemplating the mission and the fate of your captured companion. Now that it appears Magnaarn has found the Doomstone, you know you should do as Captain Prarg insisted; you should try to reach Antah and confront him before he can use his newfound power against the Lencians. But you are loath to abandon your guide. You have promised Prarg that you will help him escape and a Kai Grand Master never breaks his word. The Captain has been captured as a spy and, as such, he can expect no mercy from the Drakkarim.

Soon after dawn you witness some activity in the main square which confirms your worst fears. A squad of Drakkarim engineers arrive and set to work constructing a raised wooden platform in the centre of the square.

An hour later, when their work is complete, a covered wagon arrives. The engineers unload a large lump of black oak which they place in the middle of the platform, and, as you focus on this block, a shiver runs the length of your spine the moment you realize its grim purpose.

Turn to **109**.

73

"You will commence your mission at midnight," says the King, motioning you towards a small window which overlooks the busy harbour of Vadera. He points to a ship, one of several moored at the quayside, but one that is readily identifiable for it is the only vessel not in military service.

"That trading sloop will carry you and the Captain to the small island you can see in the distance. That is Battle Isle. There you will find a sailing boat with enough provisions for your mission. The Captain knows where it is hidden and he will be responsible for your safe passage once you set sail for the Hellswamp. Remember, secrecy is vital to the success of your mission. Trust nobody save Captain Prarg:"

The King voices his fear that Drakkarim spies are operating in the harbour and he expresses his concern that your unexpected arrival by air may have already alerted them to your presence here in Vadera. However, it is too late to change the plan; it is a risk you must accept.

Having concluded your briefing, King Sarnac sends for an escort to take you to a private chamber where you can rest and reflect upon the mission ahead. Later that evening, you and Captain Prarg are smuggled out of the citadel via a secret passage which leads directly to the harbour. Quietly you board the sloop and hide yourselves amongst its cargo of supplies which are destined for the garrison on Battle Isle. The ship sets sail on the first strike of midnight and, after a smooth and uneventful voyage, it moors at a jetty on the southern coast of Battle Isle three hours later.

The crew of the sloop are unaware that you are aboard and, in order to safeguard your secrecy, you await your chance to disembark without being seen. Soon the opportunity presents itself. As the crew go in search of help to unload the cargo, the two of you leave the sloop and hurry off along the beach, heading north towards the place where your sailing boat awaits. There is no cloud and a near-full moon illuminates the rocky beach, making it easy for you to progress despite the difficult terrain.

If you possess Grand Pathsmanship, turn to **183**.
If you do not possess this Grand Master Discipline, turn to **143**.

74

You tell the three Lencians to spread out into an extended line and watch carefully for your signals. Then you scale the river bank and make your approach to the trees. The three men all seem to be competent scouts but you have your reservations. Had it not been for Schera's insistence, you would have preferred to scout this copse alone.

You have only just entered the copse when one of the Lencians accidentally steps on a dry twig. There is a loud crack and, almost immediately, a volley of arrows comes screaming out of the trees, forcing you to throw yourself face-first into the snow to avoid being hit.

Pick a number from the *Random Number Table*. If you possess Grand Pathsmanship, add 2 to the number you have picked.

If you total score is now *4* or less, turn to **204**.
If it is *5* or more, turn to **180**.

75

The sudden jolt knocks you backwards off your horse and, as you hit the ground, you strike your head and lose consciousness. Sadly, you never reawaken. A few moments after your fall, you are mobbed by angry Drakkarim soldiers who slay you out of hand.

Tragically, your life and your quest end here in Shugkona.

76

You detect a strong presence of evil lurking somewhere nearby and you warn Prarg of what you sense. Cautiously, the two of you leave this chamber by a passage which leads to a flight of black stone steps. You ascend the steps to a domed chamber which is sheathed with dull black stone. Heavy velvet hangings of ebony hue cover most of the walls, and all of the furnishings are upholstered with the same morbid cloth. The sensation of evil is stronger here, so strong that you feel as if you are slowly suffocating.

"It's here . . . " you whisper, your hand reaching for your weapon, "The Doomstone. I can feel its presence!"

Suddenly there is a movement away to your left and a blast of white-hot energy comes roaring towards your face. You dive aside in time to avoid it, but the bolt rebounds from the steel-hard wall and glances off the back of Prarg's head, knocking him unconscious.

Turn to **145**.

77

You watch with mounting anxiety as the Drakkar officer approaches the execution block. He halts beside the helpless Captain and signals to the gaolers to step back, to give him room to enact the execution. Then he takes an oiled stone from his pocket and an ugly sneer spreads across his face as he proceeds to sharpen the blade of the great axe with slow deliberation.

If you possess Kai alchemy, turn to **123**.
If you do not possess this Discipline, turn to **229**.

78

Bravely the horse attempts to clear the trench but it is simply too exhausted to jump. Its forelegs buckle as it approaches the edge and you and Prarg are thrown head-first into the trench. Luckily, you both land in deep snow and emerge unharmed by the fall.

Turn to **250**.

79

Having finished your evening meal, you are faced with a difficult decision: who should take the first watch. Both of you are very tired, and after a whole day's rowing you are less than enthusiastic about the prospect of trying to stay awake for another four hours.

If you decide to volunteer for the first watch, turn to **277**.
If you would rather decide the matter on the toss of a coin, turn to **51**.

80

You step closer to the door and carefully examine the combination lock. You are confident that, with your skill and experience, you will soon have it open without too much difficulty.

Study the following sequence of numbers. When you think you have worked out what the missing number is turn to the page which is identical to your answer.

If you guess incorrectly, or if you cannot solve the door puzzle, turn instead to **27**.

81

The night passes without incident and you awake to a bright dawn feeling refreshed by your long, uninterrupted sleep. Prarg, too, has slept well, and he feels eager to start the journey to Shugkona. Fresh snow has fallen during the night; and when you descend to the base of the tree, you discover several sets of footprints nearby. Your pathsmanship senses tell you that they are little more than an hour old and were made by a Drakkarim patrol heading due north.

You set off towards the north east, following a frozen stream that winds its way through the forest like a glistening crystal serpent. Luck and your Kai skills keep you safe from the Drakkarim patrols, and by noon you find yourselves approaching the outskirts of Shugkona. From the cover afforded by a small wooden footbridge that crosses the icy stream, you are able to reconnoitre this heavily fortified Drakkarim town. Log-lined trenches encircle most of its perimeter, fronted by pits filled with sharpened stakes to counter attacks by enemy cavalry. Mantlets and wheeled barricades defend its four highway approaches, and the whole line is manned by squads of Drakkarim and Hammerland mercenaries. However, this formidable protection comprises just a first line of defence behind which there are more fieldworks, sharpened stakes and watchtowers, many bearing recent scars of war. The town itself lies within this second circle. It is constructed entirely of wood, and many of its outermost buildings have, over the years, been reduced to ash by Lencian firebombs. You learn from Prarg that Magnaarn's headquarters are located at the very centre, in a high tower which commands a clear view over the town and its defensive lines.

At first sight the Shugkona defences look impregnable, but after having carefully observed the perimeter lines you note two places where, with luck, you might enter the town without being observed. The first is close to the east road where an expanse of cleared ground is guarded only by a watchtower. The second is a section of the perimeter, further south, where only one line of trenches has been completed.

If you wish to try to enter Shugkona from the east, turn to **285**.

If you choose to try to enter Shugkona from the south, turn to **129**.

82

For a few moments you stare at the lifeless body of the tunnel stalker, then you sheathe your weapon and continue the chore of clearing away the rockfall. Soon you have removed enough debris to enable you to squeeze through the gap to a clear section of the stairwell beyond. Once here, you block the opening behind you, and then race up the steps to the level above.

Turn to **159**.

83

Your super-sensitive hearing detects the faint sound of stone grating on stone. Then you notice that a line of loopholes are opening at chest height along both walls of this passageway, revealing the sticky sharpened tips of venom-coated spears.

"Get down!" you shout, and throw yourself flat on to the damp stone floor. Moments later, a volley of the deadly spears comes hurtling from out of the walls to smash and splinter in the passageway. Both you and your companion escape injury, your timely warning saving you from certain death.

To continue, turn to **292**.

84

"Follow me!" shouts Prarg, and before you can stop him he is on his feet and sprinting away. Hurriedly you follow him, with the lookouts shouting wildly in your wake.

"Halt!" they scream, "Halt or we shoot!"

There is the sound of bowfire, then two arrows hit the rocks and shatter close by your feet. You invoke your Magnakai skill of invisibility to keep you safe, but your Discipline does not extend to Captain Prarg who is less than an arm's length ahead of you.

Then your senses tingle anew, drawing your eyes towards a ridge less than thirty yards from the beach. Standing there, clutching loaded crossbows, are two more Lencian lookouts.

"Beware!" you cry to Prarg, but already the Lencians are preparing to fire at your fleeing forms.

Pick a number from the *Random Number Table*.

If the number you have chosen is 0, turn to **261**.
If it is 1–3, turn to **12**.
If it is 4 or higher, turn to **155**.

85

You take a deep breath and launch yourself feet-first into the icy lake. At first, as the dark water closes over your head, your senses are numbed by the intense cold. Then your Magnakai skill of nexus begins to protect your body and the cold gives way to a warm, tingling glow.

Using your infra-vision, you detect Prarg by the warmth radiating from his body. He is caught upon a jagged ridge of ice and, as you take hold of his tunic and try to pull him free, suddenly you feel unable to move. Something has taken hold of your legs!

If you possess Magi-magic, turn to **101**.
If you do not, turn to **293**.

86

Inspired by your victory, the Lencians and their League-land allies repel the remaining Zagganozod and close their ranks until the square is intact once more. The enemy are now exhausted and wearily they retreat across the plain with the stinging cheers of their foes echoing in their ears.

Then an ominous noise comes rolling across the plain from the city of Darke, a thunderous boom that shakes the very ground on which you stand. You look towards the city and see that the battle is growing ever fiercer. But now there is a new and sinister aspect. Flickerings of magical fire can be seen dancing along battlements, engulfing friend and foe alike. You sense that it is the work of Magnaarn; he and his Nadziranim allies are responsible for this.

Then, through the smoke of battle, you see a Lencian flag flying proudly amidst the carnage that is taking place on the coastal plain to the south of the city. Here, King Sarnac's crusaders have turned an enemy flank and are storming its weakened centre. Maquin and Schera see the flag and, encouraged by the cheers of their own men, they decide to march at once in support of the crusader's brave attack.

You wish them both good fortune, for you know the time has come to part company with these brave men. Their destiny awaits them on the field of battle; yours will be found inside the city of Darke itself where, if you are to fulfil your quest, you must confront Warlord Magnaarn.

You bid them farewell and watch as they lead their men in a marching column across the plain towards the distant field of battle. When they are a mile away, you set off alone towards the hamlet, which lies en route to the gates of Darke.

Turn to **140**.

87

You enter the stables by a side door and soon find a hiding place in one of a hundred straw-filled stalls. You also find the following items which may be of use to you:

Lantern
Rope
Dagger
Enough food for 2 Meals
Hourglass

If you choose to keep any of these items, remember to adjust your *Action Chart* accordingly.

Periodically, Drakkarim enter and search the building, but they fail to detect you. While you are hiding from their search parties, you consider your companion's plight and grow ever more fearful for his safety. You are also very anxious that, under torture, he will reveal your presence, your identity and the reason why you have come to this town. You are determined not to allow this to happen and so, as midnight approaches, you slip away from your hiding place and make your way stealthily towards the Shugkona Gaol.

Turn to **236**.

88

Schera considers your question, then he replies:

''I'm sorry, I've heard nothing. There have been so many men lost, killed, or captured since Magnaarn attacked. I know of this officer, and though we've never met, I've heard tell that he is a good and brave man. All I can tell you is that I have not seen him here in Konozod.''

Turn to **214**.

89

This dry and crumbling surface is the worst you have ever attempted to climb, but it does not defeat you. Your consummate climbing skills and natural grace of movement ensure that you do not falter for a moment. You clear this section of the chasm wall and safely reach the ledge above.

Turn to **132**.

90

Your psychic attack penetrates the war-dog's mind, causing it to howl with pain and terror. Immediately the others halt in their tracks, visibly shaken by the horrible cries issuing from their leader as he rolls over and over in the snow. You sense that the pack is torn now between its desire to satisfy its gnawing hunger and its natural instinct for survival. Eventually the instinct for preservation wins out, and one by one the dogs turn and flee for the safety of the forest.

Confident that the Akataz will not be back this night, you return to the boat to catch some sleep while Prarg begins his turn on guard.

Turn to **194**.

91

From the cover of the forest's edge you observe the temple, taking in every detail, your eyes scouring every inch of its leprous grey exterior for a way of gaining entry without being detected. Much of the temple is derelict yet it is still an imposing edifice, especially the squat stone tower which stands intact at its centre. Its walls are covered with intricate designs that must have taken centuries to complete, yet while you admire the craftsmanship you find the embellishments wholly repulsive for they depict and glorify acts of great evil.

The ruins are deserted, except for a wide ramp of stone which leads to a pair of huge bronze doors set into the base of the tower. These doors are open but they are guarded by two of Warlord Magnaarn's Tukodak.

If you have Assimilance, turn to **201**.
If you do not possess this Grand Master Discipline, turn to **54**.

92

Reluctantly, you abandon your attempt to open this door and retrace your steps to the junction. Prarg leads you along the opposite passageway until you come to a corner. He turns the corner before you can warn him otherwise, and finds himself staring at the brutish features of a Drakkarim Death Knight Sergeant. The warrior's curses echo loudly along the narrow corridor as he draws his sword and comes striding towards your careless companion.

If you have a Bow and wish to use it, turn to **219**.
If you do not, or if you choose not to use it, turn to **104**.

93

Along the walkway comes a lumbering hulk with cold scarlet eyes. This beast is covered with a vile fur which glistens in the

A beast with cold scarlet eyes lumbers along
the walkway.

grey-green light of the tunnel. Its long sinewy arms are out-stretched and in both of its huge hands it holds chunks of dagger-like flint. Its bloated belly skims the floor as it stalks closer, and a brown gluey saliva bubbles and runs freely from its fanged lower jaw.

Using your Kai mastery you command this beast to halt and for a few seconds it ceases to advance, but you can sense that it is being driven by a desperate hunger, a hunger that could prove stronger than your Kai mastery.

Pick a number from the *Random Number Table*. For every level of Kai rank you have attained above Kai Grand Master Superior, add 1 to the number you have picked.

If your total score is now 5 or less, turn to **197**.
If it is 6 or higher, turn to **110**.

94

Layers of heavy snow clouds blanket the moon, and dusk quickly fades to a darkness which is total. Yet, using your Magnakai night vision, you experience no difficulties as you follow Magnaarn's tracks across the open plain.

Shortly before midnight you come to the banks of the River Shug, close to a small cluster of log huts which are grouped around a derelict ferry post. Your enemy's week-old tracks lead you to the centre of this deserted settlement.

Turn to **278**.

95

You focus on the distant mass of floating vegetation as you evoke the Brotherhood spell ''Sense Evil'' and immediately you are able to feel the presence of several hostile creatures. They are lying in ambush beneath the raft of weeds and among the dank thickets which line the adjoining bank.

You tell Prarg of what lies ahead and wisely he heeds your warn-ing. He suggests you draw in the mainsail to prevent the wind from propelling your boat any nearer to the obstruction, yet once the sail is gathered, still you find yourselves drifting inexorably towards your would-be ambushers.

If you wish to make use of the oars in order to escape from probable ambush, turn to **272.**
If you choose to do nothing further to prevent the boat from drifting towards the raft of weeds, turn to **308.**

96

The two commanders have a great respect for your Kai instincts and immediately they order their men to return to the river bank. Once you are in position, you keep your eyes glued to the north, expecting to see the appearance of the enemy at any moment. You do not have to wait too long, for within minutes of returning here, you see the first few outriders of a Drakkarim cavalry platoon crest the horizon.

You magnify your vision and recognize them to be part of Magnaarn's own army. They are carrying lances topped with pennants that bear Magnaarn's personal emblem: an eagle clasping two fiery swords. Steadily these cavalry scouts draw closer. They are riding directly towards the river.

Pick a number from the *Random Number Table*.

If the number you have picked is odd (*1, 3, 5, 7, 9*), turn to **19.**
If the number is even (*0, 2, 4, 6, 8*), turn to **242.**

97

In the distance you see a makeshift roadblock. Several trees have been hacked down and they are strewn haphazardly across the road. Behind this obstruction stand several armoured Drakkarim, waiting eagerly for you to appear.

At once, you leave the road and take cover in the forest. The trees hereabouts are too dense to allow you to enter on horseback, so reluctantly you abandon the mare and enter on foot. Your instinct and pathsmanship skills lead you in a westerly direction and you cover more than five miles before the trees begin to thin out. Then you emerge from the forest to be greeted by a spectacular sight.

Turn to **174.**

98

You reach Bear Rock shortly before dusk. The landmark is a massive granite boulder, weather-worn into the shape of a huge bear standing upright with its forepaws extended. It is positioned on the west side of the Gourneni and overshadows a sheltered cove formed where, over the centuries, the river has undercut the bank. Here you bring the boat ashore and make camp for the night.

Over your evening meal you discuss the next leg of your mission. In the morning you will hide the boat before setting off cross-country towards Magnaarn's headquarters at Shugkona. Fifty miles of dense timberland separate you from this town and, in current conditions, you estimate it will take at least two days to reach.

> If you possess Animal Mastery *and* have reached the rank of Kai Grand Guardian or higher, turn to **119.**
> If you do not possess this Discipline, or have yet to reach this level of Kai rank, turn to **79.**

99

You flatten yourself against the bottom of the rowboat and listen to the gruff voices of the Drakkarim as you draw closer to their position. You hear splashes, then suddenly there is a loud thud and the rusty tip of an arrow punches its way through the side of the boat, stopping barely inches in front of your face. You hear the enemy's coarse laughter and you realize that they are simply using your boat for a spot of target practice. They are unaware that you are hiding inside. As you drift past them they rapidly lose interest in your craft. They put down their bows, pick up their makeshift fishing lines, and resume their efforts to catch themsleves something to stave off their hunger.

Turn to **227.**

100

Although you have been greatly weakened by your internment, your powers of Nexus are still sufficient to neutralize the effects of the noxious fumes.

As your mind clears and your strength returns, you approach the circular door and take a closer look at its strange octagonal lock. It comprises a keyhole and a series of numbers, although one of the numbers is clearly missing. Experience tells you that this is a dual combination lock, one that can be opened either by key or by tapping in the correct number which is missing from the sequence.

If you possess a Green Key, turn to **273**.
If you do not, turn to **80**.

101

You look down at your feet and, using your infravision, you see the outline of a huge, slug-like amphibian poised no more than a fathom below. Wrapped tightly around your legs are two rope-like tentacles which extend from a sac beneath the creature's solitary eye. You try to kick free but it will not easily let you go. Slowly it is drawing you deeper into the lake.

Desperate to get free, you summon to mind the Elder Magi battle spell of "Concussion". Then you project your right hand at the creature and a deep boom resonates in your head, its effect greatly amplified by the water. At once the creature releases you and dives for the shelter of its lair, trailing blood from those parts of its body which pass for its ears.

Once free, you take hold of Prarg's tunic and pull him towards the jagged hole in the ice.

Turn to **281**.

102

You release your drawstring and send the arrow screaming towards the creature's hairless skull. Almost immediately it strikes the beast above its right eye and, although it does not penetrate bone, the shock of the impact knocks the Ciquali off its webbed feet and sends it tumbling backwards into the water.

You shoulder your bow and rush to help Prarg who is lying, barely conscious, with his face in the shallow water which is sloshing around at the bottom of the boat. You are reaching down to pull him over on to his back when suddenly you feel two pairs of scaly hands grab hold of your cloak. With a loud growl, you spin around and unsheathe your weapon in readiness to deal with your attackers.

They are two Ciquali, their hides decorated with ritual scars which mark them as warriors of their tribe. At first they back away, shocked by the speed of your reflexes, but rapidly their nerve returns and, half-crouched, they glare at you with their hideous, bulging eyes. Their throat sacs swell and collapse with increasing rapidity as they approach the moment to strike, then, with a shrill screech, they raise their claw-tipped hands and leap simultaneously towards your chest.

Ciquali: COMBAT SKILL 30   ENDURANCE 27

If you win this combat, turn to **313**.

103

Swiftly you rise up out of the snow and run to the tower where you meet up with Prarg at the foot of the wooden steps.

"That guard'll not be raising any alarms," he says, cocking his thumb behind him towards the tower door. "And they'll not find him too soon, neither."

You smile knowingly. Then Prarg points to an alleyway that lies sandwiched between two burnt-out hovels at the edge of the town, and suggests you go that way.

"Lead on Captain," you say, and follow as he runs towards the alley's shadowy entrance.

Turn to **162**.

104

You draw your weapon, turn the corner, and run at the Death Knight with it held ready to strike him down. The warrior meets your stare and laughs. Confidently he parries your first blow, then strikes out for your neck.

Death Knight: COMBAT SKILL 33   ENDURANCE 34

If you win this combat, turn to **173**.

105

Despite the treacherous surface, your consumate climbing skills and natural grace of movement ensure that you do not falter for a moment. You clear this section of the chasm wall and reach the base safely.

Turn to **71**.

106

Once inside the stable you discover two horses. One is old and lame, but the other is young and powerfully built. Using your powers of animal control, you subdue them and lead the younger horse, a grey mare, from its stall. As you leave the stable you see Prarg pointing frantically towards the crest of the hill. A troop of Drakkarim cavalry are descending towards the bridge.

Quickly you mount the mare and help Prarg to climb up upon her back. Then the enemy see you and immediately they sound a horn. Moments later an old Drakkar appears at the door to the cabin. He is holding a Bor musket, and when you fail to obey his command to halt, he levels his primitive gun at you and pulls the trigger.

Pick a number from the *Random Number Table*.

If it is *0–6*, turn to **131**.
If it is *7–9*, turn to **307**.

107

The Drakkar who is carrying the sack appears to be very anxious. His companion also seems wary and alert. As you are moving towards the doorway, he glimpses you and commands you to halt at once. When you do not obey, the two of them draw their swords and come running towards the doorway with their blades held ready to cut you down.

Drakkarim Escorts:

COMBAT SKILL 30   ENDURANCE 32

If you win this combat, turn to **222**.

108

You remove your hand and uncover the proud countenance of King Ulnar V stamped on the face of the coin.

"Well done, Prarg. You've guessed correctly." you say, and press the Gold Crown back into your pouch. "I'll stand the first watch—you get some sleep. We've a long march ahead of us tomorrow and you'll need all your strength."

Prarg breaths a sigh of relief, and while he settles himself down to sleep in the relative comfort of the boat, you pull your cloak about you and climb to the top of Bear Rock where you begin your lonely vigil.

For hours you sit on this windswept boulder, staring out through a curtain of swirling snow at the surrounding timberline. Despite your fatigue you stay alert and your iron discipline pays off when, shortly before midnight, you sense movement at the forest's edge. Then your super-keen Kai senses detect an animal scent on the cold air which you recognize immediately: it is Akataz.

Turn to **147**.

109

The solid lump of oak is an executioner's block. Its surface is cut and scarred by blows from a heavy axe, and its sides are stained dark with the blood of a hundred Lencian prisoners who have lost their lives upon it.

Suddenly your thoughts are disturbed by the rhythmic stamp of marching feet and your eyes are drawn to the avenue which runs

The Captian is dragged up on to the platform and is
made to kneel before the solid oak executioner's block.

alongside Magnaarn's headquarters. Down this thoroughfare come a regiment of Drakkarim. They file into the square and form up in three lines facing the platform. Then an open wagon, drawn by a brace of half-starved oxen, emerges from the alleyway beside the gaol. Captain Prarg is standing in the rear of the wagon with his hands tied behind his back. Despite the bumpy ride he stands rigidly at attention, proudly defiant in the face of imminent death. The wagon halts and the Captain is dragged up on to the platform by three brutish gaolers. He is made to kneel down before the block as a Drakkar officer hurriedly reads the contents of a scroll to the assembled troops. He is condemning the Captain to death for spying. When he finishes the reading, he takes a two-handed axe from one of the gaolers and walks slowly across the platform towards the block. Clearly he intends to carry out the execution personally.

If you have a Bow and wish to use it, turn to **244**.

If you do not possess a Bow, or do not wish to use it, turn instead to **77**.

110

Suddenly the creature's expression changes from fierce anger to stark fear. It drops its flint weapons, turns on its heel, and scurries off along the tunnel as fast as it can. Your use of Animal Mastery has been successful; it has subdued the creature's natural instincts and totally shattered its will.

Confident that it will not return, you take hold of the heavy chain and pull it to raise the grill a few feet off the walkway, just high enough for you to duck under the rusty bars and continue along this tunnel. After a few hundred yards, the tunnel turns to the south. At this point you discover a flight of slimy steps that ascend from the walkway towards a darkened arch.

If you wish to ascend the steps to the arch, turn to **30**.

If you decide to ignore the steps and continue along the tunnel, turn to **248**.

111

Your final blow kills the scarlet wasp-leader and immediately the surviving swarm members break off their attack. They stream towards the opening at the centre of the ceiling and disappear towards the sky at the top of the shaft, closely followed by the remainder of their colony.

When you feel sure that the nests are empty, you reach up and take a grip of the rough brick which lines the shaft. It offers good purchase for your fingers and toes, enabling you to climb past the nests and reach the top of the shaft in a matter of minutes.

Turn to **270**.

112

The creature utters a spine-chilling shriek as it comes bounding towards you, its sabre-like teeth glinting in the wintery sun. You step back and draw your weapon just in time to defend yourself as it makes its first strike.

Mawtaw: COMBAT SKILL 43   ENDURANCE 50

This creature is immune to the effects of Mindblast and Psi-surge. If you choose to use Kai-surge, add only 1 point to your COMBAT SKILL.

If you possess Kai-alchemy, and have reached the rank of Sun Knight (or higher), you may increase your COMBAT SKILL and ENDURANCE point scores by 5 each for the duration of this combat.

If you win this combat, turn to **22**.

113

Fifty yards along the tunnel, you turn a corner and find yourself face-to-face with a nightmarish creature. From out of the gloom comes a lumbering hulk that fixes you with its pair of hungry scarlet eyes. The beast is covered with a vile fur which glistens in the eerie half-light of the tunnel, and its long sinewy arms are outstretched as if it is sleepwalking. But this beast is not asleep. In both of its huge hands it holds chunks of dagger-like flint which it wields like weapons. Its distended belly skims the floor as it gathers speed, and a brown gluey saliva runs freely from its fanged lower jaw.

With a shriek, the creature comes lunging towards you, flailing the air with its dagger-flints as it closes in for the kill. You step back and get ready to defend yourself as the beast rushes towards you at a breathtaking pace.

Tunnel Stalker: COMBAT SKILL 43   ENDURANCE 48

If you win this combat, turn to **296.**

114

You hear approaching footsteps, then through the open archway comes a Lencian soldier attired in the parade tunic and breeches of a Court Captain. He is unusually tall, but his most striking feature is his close-set eyes which are bright above his thin, hawk-like nose and bushy black moustache.

"May I introduce you to Captain Prarg," says King Sarnac. "He will be your guide."

The Captain shakes your hand and bows his head respectfully.

" 'Tis an honour to have been the one choosen to accompany you, Grand Master Lone Wolf, on such a noble quest."

Turn to **73.**

115

You watch the Drakkarim sergeant, who is pilfering his Captain's private stock of wine, tilt the bottle back to take another long gulp. He belches loudly, then bangs in the cork and replaces the bottle on the shelf before turning to leave. You wait until he is out of view before you slip into the cabin and close the door.

You hurry to the table but, to your disappointment, the map you glimpsed earlier turns out to be merely a construction plan of the encampment. It offers no clues to Magnaarn's present location.

If you wish to search this cabin more thoroughly, turn to **309.** If you choose to leave the cabin and return to Prarg, turn to **251.**

116

You clamber over the bodies that are heaped chest-high around the shattered city gates, then you begin to fight your way steadily towards the center of this terrible stronghold. Beyond the entrance you see that a wild battle is raging through the streets. A regiment of Lencian Crusaders are fighting to wrestle possession of the keep from a determined horde of Magnaarn's Drakkarim. The tide turns against the Lencians and as they are driven back towards the gates, you are forced to climb a stair which leads to the battlements in order to avoid being lost in the crush. Halfway up the steps you are attacked by a Drakkar armed with sword and shield. You duck his clumsy swipe and lash out at his chest. He catches your blow on his shield, but the sheer force of your attack hurls him down on the steps where he remains, cradling his broken arm, tears streaming down his soot-blackened face.

You stride up the steps towards the battlements where a group of Lencians are locked in combat with two Death Knights. The Crusaders slay their enemies, but they, in turn, are slain when a bolt of crackling crimson energy rips through their shiny steel armour, fired from the tip of a wizard's staff. Their lifeless bodies come tumbling down the steps, knocking you flat on your back and pinning you down beneath the weight of their armour. You struggle to get free, but you are being observed by the one who slayed the knights: an evil Nadziranim wizard. He levels his staff at your head and a swirling trail of sparks ignites at its tip. With imminent death staring you full in the face, you steel yourself to meet your maker.

Turn to **161**.

117

You head towards an archway in the far wall, advancing with caution as you traverse the slippery mounds of rubble which litter the floor of this damp and unwholesome chamber. A short tunnel lies beyond the arch. It ends at a junction where a wider passageway crosses from west to east.

If you wish to go west, turn to **237**.
If you wish to go east, turn to **24**.

118

Whilst observing the guards, a bold idea springs to mind. You tell Prarg to take a firm grip of your cloak and stay close as you cross the clearing and approach to within twenty yards of the stone ramp. At this point you use your Discipline of Assimilance to summon a fog from out of the frozen ground. A dense white vapour arises which quickly envelops the guards before they can take steps to avoid it. Vainly, the two Tukodaks shout to each other and stab at the mist with their spears, lest an enemy should be poised to attack them. With Prarg clinging to your cloak, you slip past the confused guards with ease and make your way into the tower unseen.

Turn to **199**.

119

After your meal, you leave Prarg and climb to the top of the river bank. Here, using your Grand Mastery, you send forth a mental command into the surrounding forest, summoning creatures to your aid. At first there is no response, then a pair of white Nyras Timberwolves appear at the forest's edge and, upon your command, they approach you. Normally these wolves are wild and feral creatures, slave to nothing save their natural instincts, yet your mastery over them is total; they are utterly compliant to your will.

You command the two wolves to guard your camp while you and Prarg are sleeping. With a blink of their eyes they acknowledge your order and settle themselves on their haunches. You return to the boat and tell Prarg what you have done. At first he is sceptical, but having already witnessed some of your powers in action, he does not protest too hard, especially as he can now look forward to a long sleep without having to stand watch. Unfortunately for Prarg, his hopes for an uninterrupted night's rest are soon shattered.

Turn to **38**.

120

With mixed feelings you begin your trek through the forest. You are still hopeful of defeating Magnaarn, but you are less than enthusiastic about the prospect of having to foot-slog more than 250 miles in order to reach Darke, the city where you are most likely to find your sworn enemy.

Pick a number from the *Random Number Table*.

If the number you have picked is *0–4*, turn to **195**.
If it is *5–9*, turn to **42**.

121

You raise your weapon and strike one of the sentries a killing blow as you slam through their brave but futile defence. They are trampled under your horse's hooves and you clear the gap, but it is not until you are racing along the road beyond the barricade that you realize you have been wounded in the leg: lose 3 EN-DURANCE points.

To continue, turn to **28**.

122

The creature opens its great jaws and from the depths of its throat it coughs forth a guttering ball of flame. Immediately, your senses alert you to the fact that this is no ordinary fireball; it is wholly psychic in nature. It comes roaring towards you, like a minisun trailing fiery orange sparks, and although you try to dodge aside, it follows your feint and hits you in the back with numbing force. Unless you possess the Discipline of Kai-shield, lose 5 ENDURANCE points.

The sudden jolt knocks you to the floor. Before you fully recover your footing, the creature seizes its advantage and comes leaping through the air towards your chest.

Turn to **255**.

123

Immediately below the window of the grain tower sits a Drakkar lancer astride his warhorse. He is one of a dozen troopers who have been posted around the perimeter of the square to guard its many exits, but he is more interested in watching the execution than carrying out his duty. His lance is sheathed in a tube-like scabbard fixed to the rear of his saddle, and all his attention is focused on the platform. He is unaware that you are hiding barely a few yards from where he sits.

The officer puts away his oiled stone and a murmur of expectation ripples through the assembled Drakkarim as he gets ready to raise the axe. Captain Prarg has no more than a few minutes left to live; you must act now if you are to save him. Using a Brotherhood spell—''Mind Charm''—you will the lancer to dismount from his horse, and at once he obeys your mental command. He climbs down, and as he wanders away, you leap from the open window and land in the empty saddle. Seizing the reins you spur the horse forward and it takes off across the square at a gallop. Then you unholster the lance and bring it to bear as you race headlong towards the backs of the Drakkarim soldiers who are standing between you and the platform.

Turn to **58**.

124

You pull your cloak close about your shoulders and draw upon your camouflage skills to keep you hidden as you follow the two Drakkarim towards the town gates. Their sergeant berates them, then he orders them to assist with a new influx of Lencians, just arrived. They are all so preoccupied with their duties that they fail to see you stride confidently through the open gates and into the town. Once safely inside, you head towards a dark, deserted alleyway which is sandwiched between a stables and an armoury. From here you observe the compound with a growing anger and pity for those trapped inside. Stirred by their plight, you vow to do what you can to help these starving men. Patiently you watch and wait for the patrols to pass, then you scurry towards the compound fence, eager to make contact with the Lencians.

Turn to **136**.

125

After several minutes spent surveying the gloomy chasm, you note two promising features. One is situated fifty feet or so directly above your head. At first it merely looks like a narrow ledge of rock with a grey semi-circular shadow poised above it, but when you look closely, you see that it is the mouth of a passageway.

The second feature lies far below you. It is a large, brick-lined tunnel situated at the eastern edge of the chasm floor, through which the waters of the dark river flow away. This, too, may offer a way out of this subterranean prison.

If you wish to attempt to climb the chasm wall and enter the passageway above, turn to **202**.

If you wish to attempt to descend to the floor of the chasm and escape via the river tunnel, turn to **175**.

126

Desperately you hack and stab at the ice but it simply will not break. Reluctantly you abandon the attempt, sheathe your weapon, and run back towards the jagged hole. You have no choice now but to enter the water. Prarg will soon be beyond help if you delay much longer.

You take a deep breath and launch yourself feet-first into the icy lake. At first, as the dark water closes over your head, your senses are numbed by the intense cold. Then your Magnakai skill of

Nexus protects your body and the terrible chill gives way to a warm, tingling sensation.

Using your infra-vision, you detect Prarg by the warmth radiating from his body. He is caught upon a jagged ridge of ice and, as you take hold of his tunic and try to pull him free, suddenly you feel unable to move. Something has taken hold of your legs!

If you possess Magi-magic, turn to **101**.
If you do not, turn to **293**.

127

Within the hour the final preparations for your airborne voyage to Lencia are completed, and Lord Floras and yourself are piped abroad the *Skyrider* by Bo'sun Nolrim and his cheerful crew of dwarves. You exchange a few reminiscences with each of the jovial crewmen and cannot help but smile when they tell you how proud they feel to have been given the chance to serve you once more.

Nolrim takes the helm and you sense a vibration run down the length of the deck as he coaxes the craft's powerful engine to life. Lord Floras joins you at the prow and together you wave a farewell to Rimoah and your fellow Kai as, steadily, the *Skyrider* ascends into the crisp, wintery sky. Then, with a sudden surge of power, the keel clears the battlements of the Tower of the Sun and swiftly the monastery and its inhabitants recede into the distance.

You and your companion are escorted to a warm cabin at the bow which has been prepared especially for your passage. It is well stocked with provisions and, spread out across a grand oak table, you find several maps of Northern Magnamund. Aided by Lord Floras, you study these maps and use them to chart your course to the Lencian city-port of Vadera. Bo'sun Nolrim is informed of your chosen route and, as he sets about implementing your course, you settle back to enjoy what will be a long voyage. By your calculations, it will take thirty hours for the *Skyrider* to reach its destination.

During your voyage, Lord Floras recounts the dramatic events which have taken place in the Western Tentarias since the demise of the Darklords. Prior to their fall, the Drakkarim nations had for many centuries kept the Lencians at bay. Countless crusades had been undertaken to recapture their former lands but all had ended in costly defeat for the House of Sarnac. Then, two years ago, the tide finally turned when the King launched an invasion across the Gulf of Lencia into the lands of Zaldir and Nyras. The boldness of his strategy and the unpreparedness of his enemies combined to win for him many victories in the early months of the war. Much of Zaldir and all of southern Nyras were taken and held by his conquering knights, and now the lines of battle are drawn diagonally across the centre of Nyras, from Lake Lenag in the north to the marshland fortress of Lozonzee in the east. However, King Sarnac cannot lay claim to total victory in the south, for the cities of Shpyder and Darke have defied all his attempts at capture. Their Drakkarim garrisons have steadfastly held on to these important strongholds and, although they have been surrounded and besieged for more than a year, still they refuse to surrender.

"At present, the war is focused around the towns of Hokidat and Konozod," says Lord Floras, tracing a circle around their location on the map with the tip of his index finger. "Many battles have been fought here but victory has, as yet, eluded us. Now, with the onset of a cruel winter, our advance has ground to a halt. Maintaining the seiges at Shpyder and Darke has drained us of troops and resources that would have been put to better use in the north. To compensate for this shortage, the King has employed many companies of foreign mercenaries to reinforce his armies in the field, but their services are expensive and the campaign has already proved costly, both in revenue and lives. The King is hard pressed to pay for their continued loyalty and already several regiments have deserted. If Magnaarn were to complete his quest and strike now, whilst our battle lines are weakened, his counter-attack could push us all the way back to the sea."

Lord Floras' report is sobering, yet it serves to strengthen your determination to thwart Magnaarn's quest. Later, shortly before nightfall, you leave the cabin and go up to the stern deck for a breath of fresh air. In quiet solitude you see the great expanse of the Slovarian plain passing by more than a mile beneath the craft and, as you watch, you lose yourself in thoughts of what may await your arrival in Lencia. The night sky is clear and laced with twinkling stars. As you return to the cabin to sleep, you draw comfort from the thought that the weather and the stars have seen fit to help speed your night passage to Vadera.

Turn to **233**.

128

One of your scouts hurries to your side and takes hold of your arm, fearful that you have been mortally wounded. You pull away and brusquely you tell him that you are not seriously hurt and that he should watch where he steps in future. Sheepishly he follows as you creep forward through the snow, using the sparse undergrowth to your advantage wherever possible. You move deeper into the copse until you spy where the arrow came from. A small camp is hidden among the trees. It comprises four white canvas tents attended by a dozen lean and hungry-looking human soldiers armed with longbows. A furled battle-flag stands propped against one of the tents and you ask your scout if he recognizes its chequered black-and-white design.

"They're League-landers of Ilion," he whispers. "I know that flag well. They're good mercenaries, these men, loyal to the King. We fought alongside them at Hokidat."

You are anxious about risking another volley of arrows, but when you tell your companion of your fears, he smiles.

"Don't worry, Sire," he says, "I know how to make safe contact with them."

Turn to **7**.

129

Abandoning the shelter of the bridge, you work your way slowly along the ice-filled ditch to a point directly in front of the south trench. Here you settle to observe the Drakkarim guards who are dutifully keeping watch over this sector. All you can see of them is their brutal faces peering over the rim of their dugout, but, after a while, one by one these faces disappear. Your keen hearing detects the sound of laughter, some clicks, and a few Giak curses, and judging by what you have heard you hazard a guess that the guards are busy gambling with dice.

You decide that now would be the best time to make your move, while the guards are distracted from their duty. Prarg insists that he lead the way; he has crossed here once before and he knows a safe way through. The ground in front of the trench-line looks clear but there are concealed pits out there just waiting to snare the careless or unwary. You nod your agreement and follow in his wake as he crawls a zig-zagging route towards the distant trench.

Two minutes later you reach the mound of frost-hardened earth abutting the dugout. Silently you motion to Prarg to get ready to attack, but before he can draw his sword, one of the enemy guards pops his head up to take a cursory glance over the parapet. He is less than an arm's length from you, and his eyes and mouth spring open with sheer terror when he finds himself staring into the face of a Kai Grand Master!

Instinctively you lash out with the edge of your hand, aiming for his right temple, hoping to render him unconscious before he can warn his confederates. But the shock of seeing you makes him reel backwards, and your blow misses by a hair's breadth.

Pick a number from the *Random Number Table*.

If it is *0–6*, turn to **303**.
If it is *7–9*, turn to **148**.

130

You face the portal and shape your mouth in readiness to emit the power-word battle spell, as taught to you by your trusted friend, Lord Rimoah.

"Gloar!"

The word slams into the portal's lock like an invisible hammer before reverberating around the walls of this confined chamber. A spider's web of cracks appear in the surface of the portal and, when you place your shoulder to it and push hard, the lock breaks and the door gives way.

Turn to **10**.

131

There is a loud bang and a great grey cloud billows from the muzzle of the musket. It startles the horse, but you swiftly control the animal and urge it forwards, out on the road. Quickly you make your escape northwards, hidden from the eyes of your pursuing enemy by the acrid cloud of gunpowder smoke.

Your ears are ringing but otherwise you escape unharmed. Prarg however has not been so lucky. His arm and shoulder are bleeding from where he has been grazed by buckshot. You halt as soon as you can and, using your healing skills, you mend his wounds before continuing on your way. The use of your powers reduces your ENDURANCE points score by 3.

The mare is strong and sure-footed, and you quickly cover eight miles before you encounter something on the road ahead which makes you halt for a second time.

Turn to **97**.

132

From here you hurry into the new tunnel in search of a clear route to the surface. Unfortunately, your hopes for a quick escape are soon dashed when you arrive at a ruined staircase. It leads to a landing where you are confronted by the corpse of a Drakkarim guard, slumped beside a mound of rubble which is blocking the stairs to the level above. A quick examination of the dead body reveals that both arms are broken. Injured and trapped here by the falling rocks, it appears that this guard eventually died of thirst.

If you wish to search the body further, turn to **224**.
If you wish to attempt to clear away the rubble that is blocking the stairs, turn to **311**.

133

The bolt hits the lock and, to your horror, it rebounds and hits you full in the chest.

Pick a number from the *Random Number Table*. The number you have picked is equivalent to the number of ENDURANCE points lost as a result of this backfire (0 = 10). If you have survived this setback, make the necessary adjustment to your *Action Chart*.

Reluctantly, you abandon any thought of opening this door and retrace your steps to the junction. Prarg leads you along the opposite passageway until you come to a corner. He turns the corner before you can warn him otherwise, and finds himself staring at the brutish features of a Drakkarim Death Knight Sergeant. The warrior's curses echo loudly along the narrow corridor as he draws his sword and comes striding towards your careless companion.

If you have a Bow and wish to use it, turn to **219**.
If you do not, or if you choose not to use it, turn to **104**.

134

As your slain enemies keel over backwards and splash into the mire, you spin around to see your companion grappling with a Ciquali in a desperate hand-to-hand combat. Prarg has lost his sword and the fight is going badly for him. The creature is by far the largest of the attacking pack and much of its muscular body is protected by armour, crudely fashioned from human bones. Anxious to help your companion, you rush forward and strike the creature a mighty blow at the base of its skull, opening a fearful wound. For a few moments the Ciquali continues to fight on as if unaffected by your blow, then its webbed hands spring open, letting Prarg, who is barely conscious, fall limply to the bottom of the boat. The beast touches a hand to its shattered skull and a look of astonishment fixes upon its ugly face when it sees its gore-stained palm. You raise your weapon to strike again, to finish the creature once and for all, but a second blow proves unnecessary. Its eyes roll backwards in their sockets, then stiffly the Ciquali falls sideways over the gunwale and sinks without trace beneath the slimy water.

As one, the remaining Ciquali turn away from the boat and disappear as quickly as they had come, slipping back to the cold,

135

dark safety of their hiding places beneath the surface. Silence returns, and for a long moment you stand alert, suspecting trickery, then slowly you relax; they have gone.

Aided by your healing skills, Prarg makes a speedy recovery from the battering he sustained in combat with the Ciquali chieftain. The boat, too, has survived the attack and you are able to continue without further delay. As soon as you pass the obstruction, you hoist the sail and catch the prevailing wind which propels you northwards along the channel beyond.

You are hungry after your encounter. Unless you possess Grand Huntmastery, you must now eat a Meal or lose 3 ENDURANCE points.

To continue, turn to **98**.

135

You clamber out of the cellar and set off after the Drakkarim with weapon in hand, determined to free your companion from their clutches, but as you hurry into the western avenue you see that they have already joined with the troops who are escorting the covered wagon. The wagon has halted and you count more than fifty Drakkarim jostling the helpless Prarg, bullying and cursing him vilely. More than one voice calls out in the Giak tongue—"Let's kill the Lencian spy!"

Fearful that they are going to beat him to death, you decide to charge headlong into the crowd in a desperate attempt to save him, despite the overwhelming odds against your success. But before you can act, a Drakkar officer on horseback appears and commands the troops to order. An uneasy silence descends on the group, then dutifully they step away from Prarg and form up in a column facing the officer and his mount. Prarg, who has been left lying on the ground, barely conscious, is bundled into the wagon. The officer raises his hand and the wagon trundles off along the avenue towards a distant square, with the troop of soldiers marching smartly in its wake.

You follow and observe, taking in every aspect, every detail that might help you to free your companion. When you reach the square at the end of the avenue, you discover that it is dominated by a tall tower. It is Magnaarn's tower. His flag, emblazoned with the emblem of a black eagle clutching two fiery swords, flutters lazily from its slender wooden spire. The wagon draws up in front of a building adjacent to the tower and Prarg is dragged unceremoniously inside. Judging by the bars which adorn its windows, and the armed guards at its entrance, you hazard a guess that this is the Shugkona Gaol.

Patiently you watch the square for several minutes while you try to formulate a plan. Then the assembled troops are galvanized into action when an order from their officer sends them off in pairs to search the town for other spies. Several Drakkarim come towards your location and you are forced to seek somewhere to hide. Looking around you can see only two dwellings that may offer some hope of a safe haven. The first is a warehouse; the second a stables.

If you wish to hide in the warehouse, turn to **291**.
If you choose to hide in the stables, turn to **87**.

136

Huddled together in a corner of the compound, away from other prisoners, is a small group of men-at-arms. The fronts of their tattered blue coats bear the emblem of a crown set above the crest of Vadera identifying them to be of the same regiment—the Imperial Vadera Guard—one of Lencia's finest. Using your Magnakai skills to avoid detection, you make your way to the fence and try to attract their attention. One of their number, a Captain, sees you and is immediately suspicious. You signal to him to come closer and, reluctantly at first, he crawls towards the fence.

"You're not Drakkarim or Lencian. Who are you? What do you want?" he hisses, through cracked lips that are blue with hunger and cold. "Is this another Drakkar trick devised to torment us?"

"This is no trick," you whisper in reply, trying hard to reassure him, "I'm an ally in the service of your King. I want to help you and your men to escape."

He holds you with his steely-grey eyes and slowly shakes his head.

"It's too late to help us," he says, sadly. "We're too weak to resist. Some have tried and they've all died in the jaws of the dogs. No, you save yourself, stranger. Forget us."

"But if you stay here you'll starve to death," you retort. "Surely it's better to die fighting than waste away. The garrison here is small, barely forty in number. I could cause a diversion and draw their dogs away. Your men may be weakened but still they outnumber the enemy five times over. For Ishir's sake, man, have you lost the will to live?"

The Lencian Captain glances over his shoulder at his starving comrades and, when he turns to face you once more, you see a faint glimmer of hope in his eyes.

"All of these men have been more than a week without food or shelter. Many have died, many are near to death. I fear they are too weak to fight an enemy who has food in his belly and a sword in his hand. Perhaps . . . if we had weapons . . ."

"If you do as I say, you''ll have weapons enough to pluck this town from under their very noses," you reply, earnestly.

The Lencian narrows his eyes and, for a moment, the trace of a smile softens his gaunt features.

"Very well, stranger. Tell me your plan."

Turn to **56**.

137

Thanks to your Kai skills, the two Tukodak guards do not see you until it is too late. From the base of the stone ramp you launch a lightning attack which dispatches them both before they can attempt to raise the alarm.

Turn to **279**.

138

You utter the words of the Brotherhood spell—"Lightning

Hand''—and a crackling blast of electrical energy leaps from your fingers. The fiery bolt hits the advancing creature, stunning it momentarily, but it soon recovers and presses home its attack with renewed determination.

Turn to **267.**

139

You crash down upon the unsuspecting lancer, but the shock of impact does not unseat him and desperately he struggles to fend you off. He wounds your forearm with his sabre before you succeed in knocking him out of the saddle: lose 3 ENDURANCE points.

You seize control of the startled horse and take off across the square, unholstering the lance as you gallop headlong towards the mass of Drakkarim soldiers who stand between you and the platform.

Turn to **58.**

140

You reach the hamlet and hurry along its solitary road. Flanking you are two rows of low cottages, their thick-thatched roofs still intact despite the fiery carnage that has swept so near. Off to the right you see a barnlike building standing with its door ajar. A brazier of coals, an anvil and a scattering of iron strips prove it to have once been a busy smithy. But now, like the surrounding buildings, it is seemingly deserted.

You are passing the open door when suddenly you hear a man's voice. He has a strong Lencian accent and he is cursing you, thinking you to be a turncoat Stornland mercenary. As you turn to face the smithy door, a Lencian Crusader comes rushing out into the road, brandishing a heavy steel mace in his left hand. You yell at him that you are loyal to King Sarnac, but he ignores your plea and swings his weapon wildly at your head.

Lencian Crusader:
COMBAT SKILL 32   ENDURANCE 35

Throughout this combat you are attempting to strike a blow that will render the knight unconscious. Fight this combat using the normal combat procedure.

A Lencian Crusader rushes out into the road
brandishing a heavy steel mace in his left hand.

If you manage to reduce the knight's ENDURANCE to zero, turn to **246**.

141

For fifteen days you tunnel through a solid wall of earth and broken rock, using your weapons and bare hands, sustained all the while by little more than your indefatigable spirit and will to survive. You are near to giving up when, mid-way through the sixteenth day of your internment, you suddenly break through into a passageway that is free of debris. Weak but alive, you drag yourself into this empty tunnel and collapse on the damp, fungi-covered floor.

Reduce your current ENDURANCE points score to 15. Also, erase any Meals you may have been carrying in your Backpack, and erase any potions of Laumspur and/or Alether.

To continue, turn to **217**.

142

Captain Prarg recovers consciousness and slowly his strength returns until he is able, with your help, to regain his feet. He is cold and soaking wet, but you sense that he is no longer in a state of shock. He will survive.

Carefully you both retreat from the hole and make a wide detour around this section. An hour later you reach the far side of the lake and enter the trees beyond.

Turn to **170**.

143

You are moving across a stretch of beach which is overlooked by a small grassy hill when suddenly a harsh command splits the night air:

"Halt where you are. Do not move!"

Instantly you flatten yourself among the rocks and moments later you hear Prarg whispering. "They're Lencians. They must be lookouts from the island garrison."

Together you watch with bated breath as two inquisitive soldiers appear, silhouetted on the top of the hill. Brandishing their spears, they curse your sudden disappearance and come hurrying down a steep track towards the beach.

"Curse them," hisses Prarg, "If they find us, the whole garrison will get to hear of our mission even before it has properly begun."

If you possess Assimilance *and* you have reached the rank of Kai Grand Guardian or higher, turn to **17**.
If you do not possess this Discipline, or you have yet to achieve this rank, turn instead to **84**.

144

In order to delay the other Drakkarim, you bundle the bodies of the Death Knights down the stairs, but one soldier clambers across them and attempts to skewer you upon the tip of his spear. You sidestep his thrust and fell him with a lightning blow to the head, but not before his weapon gashes your side: lose 3 ENDURANCE points.

Hurriedly you cross to a window at the far side of the tower. Outside, directly below, you see a Drakkar lancer sitting astride a warhorse. His lance is sheathed in a tube-like scabbard fixed to the rear of his saddle and in his hand he holds aloft a heavy cavalry sabre. He is cheering those who are entering the tower and he is completely unaware that you are only a few yards away.

Swiftly you climb on to the window ledge, raise your weapon, then leap on to the unwary lancer below.

Pick a number from the *Random Number Table*. If you possess Grand Huntmastery, add 3 to the number you have picked.

If your total score is now 5 or less, turn to **139**.
If your total score is now 6 or more, turn to **26**.

145

You kneel beside Prarg and check that he is still breathing. He is fortunate that the bolt struck him a glancing blow; had it hit him squarely it would have killed him outright. Then you hear a movement over on the far side of the chamber, and when you look up, you see Warlord Magnaarn emerging from behind one of the many hanging black drapes. An aura of evil surrounds his body like a shimmering grey cocoon, and his features no longer appear as they did when first you encountered him in the subterranean labyrinths of the Temple of Antah. Now his body is twisted and mummy-like, and feverish eyes burn from black sockets within a bald skull of a face. You sense that he is wholly possessed by the object he holds clenched in his shrunken hand—the Nyras Sceptre.

The dread sceptre hums with the power of the Doomstone that is set upon its platinum shaft. Magnaarn utters an evil laugh and points the sceptre at you, but curiously you feel no weakness or leeching of strength, as occurred at Antah. The Warlord's sick eyes widen with surprise and you sense that he is fearful. He threatens you with death, but his voice is wavering. He is unsure of his power. Then you sense another presence, a magical presence. A wispy shape emerges from behind another curtain, summoned forth by Magnaarn, and at once you recognize it to be the formless life-force of a Nadziranim sorcerer. You hear Magnaarn issue a psychic command, ordering the creature to slay you, and immediately it responds. Swiftly it moves across the chamber, changing shape as it draws closer. It is no more than ten feet distant when it solidifies into a form which is truly horrifying to behold.

Turn to **39**.

146

You strike your killing blow and send the creature tumbling off the walkway into the rushing black waters of the subterranean river. It surfaces for a brief moment, its arms flailing wildly, then it disappears forever beneath the swirling foam.

Confident in your victory, you sheathe your weapon and take hold of the heavy winch chain. You pull it to raise the grill a few feet off the walkway, just high enough for you to duck under the rusty bars, then you continue along the tunnel at a brisk pace. After a few hundred yards, the tunnel turns to the south. At this point you discover a flight of slimy steps that ascend from the walkway towards a darkened arch.

If you wish to ascend the steps to the arch, turn to **30**.
If you decide to ignore the steps and continue along the tunnel, turn to **248**.

147

Quickly you return to the boat and attempt to awaken your companion. But he does not respond at once, and you are forced to shake him vigorously by the shoulders until finally he stirs to consciousness.

"Wha. . . . what's wrong!" he mumbles, as he struggles to free himself from your firm grip.

"Wake up Captain," you retort, "there's trouble coming our way."

The word "trouble" galvanizes Prarg into action. He throws off his blankets, unsheathes his sword, and follows as you lead the way up the river bank. When you reach the crest, you see a dozen or more of the leathery black war-dogs come slinking out of the trees. Your senses are drawn to one of the red-eyed creatures, who instinctively you recognize as the leader of this pack, and suddenly you recall from past experience that Akataz are susceptible to psychic attacks. Using your Magnakai abilities, you focus on this leading hound and prepare to launch a burst of psychic energy directly at its mind.

Pick a number from the *Random Number Table*. If you possess Kai-surge, add *4* to the number you have picked.

If your total score is now 6 or less, turn to **220**.
If it is 7 or more, turn to **90**.

148

The guard crashes to the bottom of the trench, but before he can raise the alarm, you and Prarg are in the dugout beside him with your weapons drawn ready to strike.

Your attack is swift and deadly. In less than five seconds, you and your companion dispatch all four of the Drakkarim trench-troopers who occupy this position, overcoming them before they can even unsheathe their swords.

Keen to maintain your advantage of surprise, you quickly leave the trench and rush across the remaining strip of open ground which separates you from the town's outlying dwellings. Prarg points ahead, to an alleyway that lies sandwiched between two burnt-out hovels, and immediately you follow as he rushes towards its shadowy entrance.

Turn to **162**.

149

Despite its fatigue, the horse clears the trench and carries you safely beyond range of the Drakkarim archers. For half a mile you skirt along the edge of the Tozaz forest, then, the moment the enemy are lost to sight, you rejoin the road and make your escape northwards.

Turn to **208**.

150

As you step away from the dead guards, you hear shouts of alarm outside the building: the roof of the stables has just erupted into a sheet of flame. The garrison is thrown into a state of near-panic as they try to fight the fire and contain the horses which are stampeding through the streets.

You run the length of the armoury and hurriedly lift the massive drawbar which holds the main doors closed. Outside, you see the perimeter guards are abandoning their posts in order to fight the fire now raging through the stables. The Lencians are on their feet. They are grouped by the entrance to the compound and, as the last of the guards leaves, they rush forward and barge open the gates. Led by the Captain, they come streaming across the flagstoned square towards the armoury, sweeping aside any Drakkarim foolish enough to try to turn this vengeful tide. With a cheer they pour into the armoury and equip themselves with weapons from its many racks of spears and swords.

"Let's take this town!" shouts the Captain, and amid stirring battle-cries of "Lencia" and "For the House of Sarnac," the starving Lencians set off to obey his command.

You try to reach the Captain, whose name you learn is Schera, but before you reach him you are swept out into the street and carried along by this crowd of battle-hungry soldiers.

Turn to **36**.

151

You breathe the words of the Brotherhood spell "Halt Missile" and, in an instant, the first of the bolts freezes in mid-air. This swift action saves Prarg from being hit, but it does not stop the second missile from striking home. Red-hot pain flares up your arm as the iron-tipped bolt gouges a deep furrow of flesh from the back of your wrist: lose 4 ENDURANCE points.

The lookouts fumble with their crossbows, desperate to fire again, but before they can reload you have disappeared along the beach. Shortly you reach a small secluded cove where Prarg discovers a rusty anchor. It is a landmark, left on purpose by agents of King Sarnac to point the way to the cave where they have left your boat and provisions. You find the cave and together you haul the boat down the beach and raise its coal-black sail before pushing it out into the icy waters of the Tentarias.

Once aboard, you trim the sail whilst Prarg takes charge of the rudder. There is a good wind and within minutes your tiny craft is bobbing towards the far western channel of the Hellswamp, twenty miles distant. You ask Prarg if this dark estuary has a name, and he replies, "Yes. The Drakkarim call it 'Dakushna's Channel' after the Darklord who once commanded the city-fortress of Kagorst. They say it is a fitting dedication, for the waterway is as deadly and as treacherous as the creature after whom it is named."

Turn to **55**.

152

You hold the bird with a mental command and use your skill to converse with it. Its response is rudimentary, but you are able to understand that many warriors, dressed in metal and riding horses, are approaching the river from the north.

You tell Captain Schera and Baron Maquin of what you have gleaned from the bird, and the Baron says, "It sounds to me that a troop of Drakkarim cavalry are coming this way."

The Captain agrees, and both commanders pass the word to their men to stay hidden and keep completely silent.

Turn to **65**.

153

The spear-wielding guard notices the Signet Ring and immediately his suspicions melt away. The ring must denote a very high rank or office within Magnaarn's army for the Tukodaks both stand rigidly to attention and bow their heads reverently. You approach the open doors and hastily they step aside to allow you and Prarg entry to the temple. Once safely inside, you cause your features to revert to normal before you set off on your urgent hunt for the Doomstone of Darke.

Turn to **199**.

154

You quickly draw an arrow and take aim through a hole in the portcullis, but the Tukodaks cower behind Prarg, using him as a human shield. Again the cruel voice booms out: "Put down your bow, Lone Wolf, or I'll have my guards kill your companion."

At once your anger subsides. You sense that this is no idle threat and, reluctantly, you obey the command.

Turn to **181**.

155

The iron-tipped bolts scream towards you but your swift reflexes are more than a match for these deadly missiles. You open your hand and thrust your palm into Prarg's back, pushing him forward and saving him from the first bolt; then you sidestep to avoid being hit by the second. The lookouts fumble with their crossbows, desperate to fire again, but before they can reload you have disappeared along the beach.

Shortly you reach a small secluded cove where Captain Prarg discovers a rusty anchor. It is a landmark, left on purpose by agents of King Sarnac to point the way to the cave where they have left your boat and provisions. You find the cave and together you haul the boat down the beach and raise its coal-black sail before pushing it out into the icy waters of the Tentarias.

Once aboard, you trim the sail whilst Prarg takes charge of the rudder. There is a good wind and within minutes your tiny craft is bobbing towards the far western channel of the Hellswamp, twenty miles distant. You ask Prarg if this dark estuary has a name, and he replies, ''Yes. The Drakkarim call it 'Dakushna's Channel' after the Darklord who once commanded the city-fortress of Kagorst. They say it is a fitting dedication, for the waterway is as deadly and as treacherous as the creature after whom it is named.''

Turn to **55**.

156

You crash down upon the unsuspecting lancer and send him tumbling from the saddle. The impact leaves him stunned, but before he can recover, you seize control of his horse and take off across the square. With your left hand you unholster the lance and bring it to bear as you gallop headlong towards the backs of the Drakkarim soldiers who are standing between you and the platform.

Turn to **58**.

157

Aided by your Kai skills, you uncover some tracks frozen beneath the snow. They were made by horses and wagons and are a little over a week old. There are far more than you expected to find here, and you can tell at once that they were not all made by Magnaarn's entourage. Before he left this site and headed west, he was joined by several hundred reinforcements.

During your search you also discover some scraps of food which you eat immediately: restore 3 ENDURANCE points. Having satisfied your curiosity, and your rumbling stomach, you decide to leave the campsite and follow the tracks westward.

If you possess Animal Mastery, and have reached the rank of Kai Grand Guardian (or higher), turn to **205**.
If you do not possess this Discipline, or have yet to reach this level of Kai training, turn to **120**.

158

The creature is badly wounded but its powerful natural psychic skills block out the pain, enabling it to press home its attack.

Turn to **267**.

159

Quickly you climb the stairs, spurred on by the wintery chill which grows steadily colder as you ascend. You count one hundred and fifty steps before you arrive at a chamber which is heaped with rubble. Its only door is blocked by debris and huge slabs of marble, making an immediate exit impossible. But it is not the door which commands your attention; it is a narrow circular shaft which is set into the middle of the ceiling. It is the source of the cold, wintery draft.

Expectantly, you step closer and investigate this shaft. For the most part it is dark, but you can see glimmers of grey daylight high above, and you can hear the whistling of the wind. But you can also hear another sound, one that is quite unexpected. It is a buzzing, insectile noise. You focus upon the darkness and suddenly you see that the noises come from nests of winged insects which are fixed to the inside of the shaft.

If you possess Grand Pathsmanship, and have reached the rank of Sun Knight, turn to **218**.
If you do not possess this Discipline, or have yet to reach this level of Kai rank, turn to **253**.

160

As the few remaining pack survivors slink away into the forest, you help Prarg, who has sustained several deep wounds to his arms and legs, to reach the boat. Repeatedly he apologizes for having fallen asleep while on guard but you refuse to let him take all of the blame.

Using your inate Kai skills you tend to Prarg's injuries and ensure that they heal without infection. He recovers quickly, but the use of your curing skills leaves you feeling weak and tired: lose 5 ENDURANCE points.

Turn to **194**.

161

Suddenly the evil wizard cries out in pained surprise and throws his claw-tipped hands into the air. A sparkling bolt, which was destined to seal your doom, arcs from his staff and blows a man-sized hole in the wall of the fortress. As the resultant smoke and dust slowly clears, you see Captain Prarg standing over the body of the slain wizard with a bloodied sword held in his hand. With a cry of victory, he leaps over the crumpled corpse and comes rushing down the steps to help free you from the tangle of bodies.

"Well met, Sire," he says excitedly. "I feared you were dead and buried at the Temple of Antah."

"I, too, thought you dead, Prarg," you reply, thankful to see him still alive. "Yet it seems that fate has decreed otherwise."

"I was lucky," he says, "I escaped from Magnaarn. But come, Sire. There's no time for tales now. We must away from here. Follow me, I know where the Warlord is hiding."

Turn to **33**.

162

The dark alleyway leads to a square where, an age ago, the grand mansions of Lencian noblemen encircled a shrine dedicated to the Goddess Ishir, High Priestess of the Moon. But now this square,

Captain Prarg stands over the body of the slain wizard
with bloodied sword in hand.

163

in common with the rest of the town, bears little resemblance to, or trace of, its Lencian origins. When the Drakkarim first captured Ferndour, as it was then called, all the houses and public buildings which had stood for centuries were demolished. In their place were erected ungainly dormitories and ugly communal dwellings made entirely of timber culled from the surrounding forest. The town's once-picturesque plazas and narrow, winding streets were replaced with coldly functional military avenues for the marching Drakkarim hordes.

From the shadows of a doorway, you and Prarg observe a small covered wagon and a troop of weary Drakkarim soldiers entering the square from the north. This small procession swings right and approaches an avenue which exits the square, leading off to the west towards the centre of the town. Magnaarn's headquarters are located in the middle of Shugkona and, with night fast approaching, Prarg suggests you follow the troop using the gathering darkness for cover. You are about to agree with him when suddenly the door of a nearby hovel swings open, and out into the alley step three burly, drunken Drakkarim.

Instinctively you both leap for cover to avoid being seen. Prarg drops down behind a stack of empty ale casks, whilst you dive behind a mound of rotten timbers. The moment you hit the ground you feel it sag beneath your weight, then, in a moment of terror, the ground collapses and you fall headlong into darkness. You have crashed through the rot-infested timbers of a trapdoor into a damp and dingy cellar.

Pick a number from the *Random Number Table*. If you possess Grand Huntmastery, add 1 to the number you have picked.

If your total score is now 0–4, turn to **215**.
If it is 5 or higher, turn to **53**.

163

You clear the gap with one bound, and even manage to stay on your feet when you land on the far side of the fissure. Hungry for victory and vengeance, you tear aside the curtain through which Magnaarn disappeared and discover a short flight of steps which emerge at a turret at the very top of the Palace Tower, the highest point in the city of Darke.

Here you find Magnaarn, cowering with his crooked back pressed hard against the frost-covered wall. You sense that he has very nearly succumbed to the evil power of the Doomstone; he is treading a fine line between life and undeath. Yet, even though he is but a whisker away from eternal damnation, he musters enough spite to challenge you to a fight to the death.

"Very well, Drakkar," you reply. "Let battle commence."

Warlord Magnaarn *(with Nyras Sceptre)*:
COMBAT SKILL 48   ENDURANCE 36

If you win this combat, turn to **314**.

164

With lightning speed you draw and fire two arrows, sending the shafts whistling deep into the scaly bellies of the two swamp creatures. Their effect is swift and deadly; the Ciquali screech in unison and throw their arms wide as they are hurled backwards into the mire. You string another arrow and glance over your shoulder at your companion who, having lost his sword, is now grappling with a Ciquali in a desperate hand-to-hand combat.

The fight is going badly for Prarg. The creature is by far the largest of the pack and much of its muscular body is protected by armour, crudely fashioned from human bones. Anxious to help your companion, you raise your bow and take aim, but the two are entwined and you dare not fire for fear of hitting the Captain. Then a sudden swipe of the creature's horny fist knocks Prarg to his knees, allowing you a moment's unobstructed view of his adversary.

If you wish to fire at the creature's head, turn to **102**.
If you choose to fire at the sac which surrounds the creature's throat, turn to **35**.
If you decide to fire at the creature's upper chest, turn to **206**.
(Remember to erase three arrows from your quiver.)

165

You hurry along this wind-swept passageway until you come to a corner. Prarg turns the corner before you can warn him otherwise, and he finds himself staring at the brutish features of a Drakkarim Death Knight Sergeant. The warrior's curses echo along the corridor as he draws his sword and comes striding towards your careless companion.

If you have a Bow and wish to use it, turn to **219**.
If you do not, or your choose not to use it, turn to **104.**

166

The arrow flies true, but at the very last moment before impact, the Drakkar spins around to face the assembled soldiers and your shaft shatters harmlessly upon the blade of his axe. For a few seconds he is stunned by the nearness of your attack, then suddenly he points to the grain tower and begins to scream like a madman:

"Up there! At the window! The arrow was fired from up there!"

Turn to **230**.

167

On reaching the main street, you see Captain Schera beckoning to you from the doorway of a ruined inn.

"Over here," he calls, "I think I've found something."

"What is it?" you say, on entering the fire-ravaged ruins.

"Come and take a look for yourself," he replies, and takes you to a flight of stone steps which lead down into a cold, dark cellar.

Turn to **178**.

168

The chieftain bellows its death cry and keels over backwards to hit the water with a mighty splash. Now leaderless, the remaining Ciquali turn away from the boat and disappear as quickly as they had come, slipping back to the cold, dark safety of their hiding places beneath the surface. Silence returns, and for a long moment you stand alert, suspecting trickery, then slowly you relax; they have gone.

Aided by your healing skills, Prarg makes a speedy recovery from the battering he sustained in combat with the Ciquali chieftain. The boat, too, has survived the attack and you are able to continue without further delay. As soon as you pass the obstruction, you hoist the sail and catch the prevailing wind which propels you northwards along the channel beyond.

You are hungry after your encounter. Unless you possess Grand Huntmastery, you must now eat a Meal or lose 3 ENDURANCE points.

To continue, turn to **98**.

169

Quickly you tend to your companion's wound, using your Magnakai curing skills to neutralize the venom before it does its fatal work. Your swift action saves him but it drains you of energy: lose 2 ENDURANCE points.

To continue, turn to **292**.

170

You move deeper into the forest, maintaining a steady pace. Here, in this part of the Tozaz, the snowfall underfoot is light because of the canopy of thick branches overhead, and you make good progress. You have been walking for an hour when a shivery rustle brings you abruptly to a halt. You look up and a miniature snowslide falls from a branch overhead, covering your face and shoulders with a deluge of powdery snow. Prarg laughs as he watches you spluttering, and as you wipe your eyes, you glimpse a grey-winged bird fluttering away to the west.

"By the Gods, I'm hungry," exclaims Prarg, leaning weakly against a tree trunk. "What I'd give for a side of beef and a plate of boiled beets."

The Captain has not eaten since before you reached Shugkona and you can see that after the rigours of his capture and escape, he is sorely in need of food. Unless he eats soon he will be unable to go much further.

If you possess a Meal, turn to **63**.
If you do not, turn to **254**.

171

You awake at first light and make a search of all the cabins, but they have either been despoiled by Giaks or stripped bare and you discover nothing of practical use. However, you do uncover enough scraps of food, preserved by the cold, to make quite a decent breakfast: restore 3 ENDURANCE points.

After your meal, you gather together your equipment and set off along the river bank, heading west. The surrounding landscape is a harsh black and white desolation, devoid of all colour. The bleakness is deepened by the constant moaning wind and the occasional cawing of distant carrion crows. Five miles downstream you happen upon a hut at the edge of the river. You are expecting it to be empty, like the others at the ferry stage, so it comes as a welcome surprise to find it contains a rowboat and a pair of oars, both in good condition. Heartened by your discovery, you launch the boat into the water and begin your voyage towards Darke.

Pick a number from the *Random Number Table*.

If the number you have picked is *0–4*, turn to **67**.
If it is *5–9*, turn to **263**.

172

Prarg makes a wide detour to the west in order to avoid the risk of walking straight into the arms of your enemies. The detour takes you across a steep and rugged part of the forest previously unexplored by your guide, and progress here is slowed dramatically. You have covered less than six miles when the failing light, and the increasing sightings of Drakkarim patrols, forces you to halt and make camp for the night.

From the safety of a treetop, fifty feet above the forest floor, you rope yourself to the trunk before settling down to sleep. You are hungry and, unless you possess the Discipline of Grand Hunt-mastery, you must now eat a Meal or lose 3 ENDURANCE points.

Turn to **81**.

173

You leap over the corpse and run down the corridor with Prarg close on your heels. Soon you reach a junction where you are forced to choose a direction, left or right. You call upon your Kai skills and immediately you sense a strong presence of evil lurking at the end of the right-hand passage. You focus on the source of this evil and determine that it is the Doomstone. You tell Prarg and together you advance along the passage until you reach a closed door.

If you possess Grand Huntmastery or Grand Pathsmanship, turn to **193**.

If you possess neither of these Disciplines, turn to **207**.

174

Before you lies a vast frozen lake, more than a mile wide at the point at which you now stand. An icy wind whips across its glistening surface, stirring freshly fallen snow into eddies which whirl and dance like spinning tops. Silently you stare across the lake at the distant tree line and your mind is filled with doubt. The Temple of Antah lies beyond, of that you are sure, and the quickest way to reach it would be to traverse the lake, but there is no cover and no way of knowing if the ice is thick enough to support you all the way across. Yet, to go around the lake would delay you by hours, giving your pursuers ample time to catch up and attack.

At length you decide to take your chances and cross the lake. At first the going is smooth and you make easy progress, but as you near the centre, suddenly you sense that something is wrong.

If you possess Grand Pathsmanship *and* have reached the Kai rank of Sun Knight or higher, turn to **50**.

If you do not possess this skill, turn to **34**.

175

You begin the descent and soon discover that the rough chasm wall makes for an ideal climbing surface. With confidence you descend towards the river, but you are almost caught unawares when you reach a section of the chasm wall which is treacherous in the extreme. It is smooth, dry and crumbly, making it suddenly impossible for you to find safe purchase for your toes and fingers.

Pick a number from the *Random Number Table*. If you have Grand Huntmastery, add 2 to the number you have picked. If you possess a Rope, add 1. If your present Kai rank is Grand Guardian or higher, add 1.

If your total score is now 6 or less, turn to **189**.
If it is 7 or more, turn to **105**.

176

As the deadly shafts scream towards you and Prarg, you open your hand and thrust your palm into his back, pushing him aside. This swift action saves him from the first bolt, but it robs you of time in which to react to the second. It strikes and red-hot pain flares up your leg as the iron-tipped bolt gouges a deep furrow of flesh from the back of your calf: lose 4 ENDURANCE points.

Turn to **55**.

177

Your keen senses detect an unpleasant odour wafting towards you on the damp air. It is the scent of a hostile animal. It is not lurking in this chamber but it is somewhere close by.

Cautiously you head towards an archway in the far wall, taking great care not to fall as you traverse the slippery mounds of rubble which litter the floor of this dank and unwholesome chamber. A short tunnel awaits you beyond the arch. It ends at a junction where a wider passageway crosses from west to east.

The animal odour is stronger here; it is wafting from out of the west tunnel. Forewarned, you shun this tunnel and set off to the east.

Turn to **24**.

178

In a corner of the cellar you see two booted and bloodstained feet protruding from beneath a mass of collapsed flooring. You move closer and discover they belong to a Lencian soldier who is badly wounded and barely conscious. Schera helps you to clear away the charred timbers that are pinning him to the ground and, using your Kai healing skills, you attend to the man's wounds. After a few minutes he recovers consciousness just long enough to tell you his name—Hul Sendal.

You both carry the man back to the river and place him carefully into your boat. The Captain's men have managed to clear a passage wide enough for the flotilla to pass through in single file, and as you continue your journey down-river, you spend some time nursing the injured soldier back to consciousness. He tells you of the battle that destroyed his regiment, of how Magnaarn used his sceptre to set the town ablaze, and of how he has survived the last six days sustained by nothing more than a few handfuls of snow. His account of the battle is chilling and it leaves you with a gnawing fear that maybe it is already too late to prevent Warlord Magnaarn from regaining control of Darke.

Turn to **188.**

179

You unsheathe your weapon and rush forward to strike the soldier down, determined to finish him quickly before he can raise the alarm.

Drakkarim Sergeant:
COMBAT SKILL 32   ENDURANCE 29

Due to the speed of your attack, ignore any ENDURANCE loss you may sustain in the first round of this combat.

If you win the combat, turn to **48**.

180

The arrows miss you by an arm's length, but as you hit the ground you gash the palms of your hands on the trunk of a fallen tree: lose 1 ENDURANCE point.

Turn to **128**.

181

From out of the shadows of the secret passage steps Warlord Magnaarn. He is a huge man—not much over six feet tall, but massively built. His body is sheathed in finely crafted armour that fits his frame like a glove, and his features are coarse and foreboding, accentuated by a fresh battle scar which runs diagonally from the top his red-haired scalp to a point near the lobe of his left ear.

Arrogantly he approaches the porticullis and stares unblinkingly into your eyes. For a moment you consider attacking him, but your senses detect that he is surrounded by a field of energy so strong that already you feel it leeching your psychic powers. He reaches to a pocket inside his cloak and takes out a large black gemstone, which he holds level with his sneering face. Scarlet veins glow within the depths of this stone, swirling and undulating as if they are alive. Waves of dizziness force you to your knees as the evil power of the Doomstone of Darke washes over you, bleeding you of the strength and will to resist.

The massively built Warlord Magnaarn steps out of the
shadows and stares arrogantly into your eyes.

"I've been waiting for you, Lone Wolf," says Magnaarn, with a condescending tone. "I've known your plan ever since my spies told me of your arrival at Vadera. After all, there could be but one reason why the great Grand Master of the Kai would come to Lencia at this time. Yet, as you can see, Grand Master, you are already too late to stop me."

Magnaarn turns to his Tukodak guards and orders them to take Prarg away. You try to protest but you cannot find strength enough to voice the words. The warlord smiles at your weakness.

"Know you this, Grand Master. Now that I possess the stone of power, nothing can stand in my way. You were the only threat to my victory, but now you're a threat no longer."

With this he steps away from the portcullis and turns to follow his guards as they drag Prarg into the secret passage.

"Farewell," he says, sardonically, before disappearing into the portal, "and remember my first words to you: welcome to your tomb."

With these chilling words echoing in your mind, you watch as he disappears into the passage and the wall closes behind him.

Turn to **40**.

182

Your arrow strikes with deadly accuracy. The Drakkar officer drops the axe and clutches the shaft which has suddenly buried itself in his throat. He tries to scream, but the arrow has destroyed his larynx and slowly he topples from the platform without uttering a sound. For a few moments the assembled Drakkarim are transfixed by his death, then a solitary voice shrieks in alarm: "Up there! The arrow came from up there!"

Turn to **302**.

183

Your super-keen senses alert you to something on the brow of a hill which overlooks this stretch of beach. You detect the faint glint of moonlight on steel and at once you whisper a warning to Prarg. Instantly he takes cover among the rocks and together you watch with bated breath as two inquisitive Lencian lookouts leave their post and come down to the sea's edge. They scan the beach then, shaking their heads, they turn and retrace their steps, pausing to skewer a few clumps of seaweed with their spears as they trek back to their post.

As the lookouts climb the hill, you and Prarg hurry away whilst they have their backs turned.

Turn to **247.**

184

With the caustic stench of your smouldering cloak filling your nostrils, you kneel before the portal and set to work in an attempt to pick its ancient lock. The mechanism is quite basic and it takes you less than a minute to pick it successfully.

However, before you escape from this chamber, the deluge of acid takes its toll upon your backpack and equipment. Erase from your *Action Chart* those items which you have recorded as the first and fourth on your list of Backpack Items. Also, erase either one Special Item of your choice, or (if you possess one) your Bow.

Turn to **10.**

185

A bold idea springs to mind. Using your Kai Discipline, you cause your facial features to take on the harsh countenance of a Drakkar warrior. At first Prarg is alarmed by your dramatic change and he steps back aghast, but you quickly reassure him that the effect is temporary; it is part of your plan to gain entry to the temple.

Prarg will act as your prisoner while you pretend to be a Drakkar guard, summoned from Shugkona by Warlord Magnaarn himself. Prarg agrees to the plan and he places his hands behind his back, as if they are tied, and you escort him towards the temple doors. As you approach the two guards you call out to them, speaking in Giak, saying that Warlord Magnaarn has sent for this prisoner. Visibly they hesitate. They have no knowledge of their master's request and are suspicious. As you ascend the ramp, one of the guards levels his spear and points it threateningly at your chest.

If you possess a Signet Ring, turn to **153**.
If you do not possess this item, turn to **52**.

186

Your acute hearing detects the faint sound of stone grating on stone. Then you notice that loopholes are opening at chest height along both walls of the passageway, revealing the sticky sharpened tips of venom-coated spears.

"Get down!" you shout, and throw yourself flat on to the damp stone floor. Moments later, a volley of the deadly spears comes hurtling from out of the walls to smash and splinter in the passageway. Your timely warning saves you and Prarg from certain death, yet, unluckily, one of the speartips ricochets and gouges Prarg's shoulder.

Turn to **169**.

187

You utter the words of the Brotherhood spell "Lightning Hand" and point the index finger of your right hand at the circular keyhole. A tingling sensation engulfs your entire arm, then a shudder runs from your shoulder to your fingertip, culminating in a burst of blue-white energy which arcs towards the lock.

Pick a number from the *Random Number Table*. If your current ENDURANCE points score is 20 or higher, add 1 to the number you have picked.

If you total score is now 7 or less, turn to **133**.
If it is 8 or more, turn to **231**.

188

West of Odnenga, the river meanders very little as it crosses the snow-swept plain of Southern Nyras. It is a deserted landscape, yet Captain Schera cautions his men to remain watchful, doubly so whenever the boats pass an occasional copse of fir or stunted pine. Late in the afternoon, as the light is beginning to fade, you come to a forested part of the river where the banks are steeply undercut. Trees are growing at the very edge of the overhanging banks and their roots are clearly visible, hanging down like clusters of vines into the icy waters of the Shug. You are watching the left bank when suddenly your pathsmanship senses alert you to the threat of ambush. You warn the Captain and he signals to the following boats to put ashore at once.

Having sensed the threat, you volunteer to go forward and scout the woods to find out who, or what, is there. Schera agrees, and he calls for three of his men, all trained army scouts, to accompany you. He and the rest of his command will remain here with the boats and wait for you to return.

Pick a number from the *Random Number Table*. If you possess Grand Pathsmanship, add 3 to the number you have picked.

If your total score is now *4* or less, turn to **74**.
If it is *5* or more, turn to **249**.

189

You have almost overcome this treacherous section of the chasm wall when a sudden slip ends in disaster. You are stretching to reach an outcrop of rock with your left hand when the powdery wall gives way beneath the toe of your left boot. You try to recover but it is too late. You slip sideways and topple head-first into the chasm where you land amongst the boulders and debris embedded into the river bank. Death is instantaneous.

Tragically, your life and your quest end here in the deepest reaches of the Temple of Antah.

190

You rush towards your stricken companion, unshouldering your backpack as you run. Once you are as close to the hole as you dare go, you tear open the pack and take out your coiled rope. Prarg is foundering in the icy water; he can barely keep his head above the surface. Hurriedly you hurl one end of the rope towards him and he makes a desperate grab for it with numbed fingers. Miraculously he grips it first time and manages to hold on tight as you haul him out of the freezing water.

His skin is violet and his entire body is shaking uncontrollably. Using your healing skills, you transmit some of your body warmth through your hands to his chest and face and, within a few minutes, he comes out of his state of shock and his body returns to its normal temperature. Your prompt action has saved his life, but it has also drained you of 3 ENDURANCE points.

Turn to **142.**

191

You swallow hard and within a few seconds you feel your strength returning. You shake your head and as your vision clears you approach the circular door and take a closer look at its strange octagonal lock. It comprises a keyhole and a series of numbers, although one of the numbers is clearly missing. Experience tells you that this a dual combination lock, one that can be opened either by key or by tapping in the correct number which is missing from the sequence.

If you possess a Green Key, turn to **27.**
If you do not, turn to **80.**

192

You sift through the items stacked upon the shelves, packed in cases and hidden in the personal bags of the Drakkarim commander, and discover the following which may be of use to you during your mission:

Dagger
Sword
2 potions of Laumspur (each restores 4 ENDURANCE points)
Hourglass
Signet Ring
Bow
3 Arrows
Brass Key

If you decide to keep any of the above, remember to make the necessary adjustment to your *Action Chart*.

To continue, turn to **251**.

193

Your Kai sense detects that your approach to this door has set off a trap.

You shout a warning to Prarg, and he reacts with commendable swiftness. The two of you hit the floor and, moments later, several razor-sharp sword blades lunge from slits in the walls to rake the air just a few feet above your heads. Then they retract and lock back into the walls with a deadly slickness.

When you are sure that this trap no longer poses a threat to your lives, you get to your feet and move forward to take a closer look at the door.

Turn to **275**.

194

You wake with the dawn and fix a hasty breakfast before breaking camp. Within the hour you are ready to begin your trek towards Magnaarn's stronghold at Shugkona, but first you must dispose of your boat. Prarg takes what provisions he needs, then, with his sword, he pierces several holes in the keel. You launch the boat towards the centre of the river and watch as slowly it sinks beneath the surface. The moment it disappears, you leave the river's edge and set off into the trees.

Deep in the forest the snowfall is light underfoot, because of the thick canopy of branches overhead, and you find the going much easier than expected. You are struck by the unexpected beauty of this dense timberland in winter, by the intricate webs of frost that trail between its blue-green branches, and by its frozen streams and waterfalls. But even as you admire it, you remain ever-conscious of its dangers. Prarg leads the way, and swiftly you progress from one concealed marker to another, all having been placed by him on previous missions behind enemy lines. By using his system of hidden signposts he is able to guide you safely through a maze of Drakkarim outposts and patrol routes that riddle this timberland.

It is nearing noon and you have covered more than twenty miles when Prarg motions you to halt: he has found something unexpected. Nailed to a trunk is a small rectangle of orange-coloured metal.

"This is a Drakkarim marker," he says, after closer examination. "They use them to mark the perimeter boundaries of their forest camps. It wasn't here the last time I came this way which means there must be a new outpost here, somewhere close."

"How close?" you ask.

"Within half a mile at most."

For a few moments you stop and listen to the silence of the forest. You close your eyes and concentrate, and through the use of your aural skills, you detect noises away to the north. The sounds are mixed and many, and you are unable to discern their exact cause.

If you wish to investigate these sounds, turn to **60**.
If you choose to avoid them, turn to **172**.

195

With forbearance, you make the difficult trek westwards through the dense forest, following the scant trail left by Magnaarn's troops. Dusk arrives within the hour and with it comes a fresh fall of snow which hampers your progress further. You are hungry, and unless you possess the Discipline of Grand Huntmastery, you must now eat a Meal or lose 3 ENDURANCE points.

To continue, turn to **94**.

196

The beast's albino eyes widen and you feel a wave of psychic energy washing over you. It is trying to subdue you, to hypnotize you. Your Magnakai skill of Psi-screen blocks this primitive mindforce but Prarg succumbs to the hypnotic suggestion. Rigidly he stands to attention as the creature makes its attack.

If you possess Animal Mastery, and wish to use it, turn to **297**.
If you possess Kai-surge, and wish to use it, turn to **8**.
If you possess Kai-alchemy, and wish to use it, turn to **138**.
If you have none of these skills, or choose not to use any of them, turn instead to **112**.

197

The creature shakes its ghastly head and emits a piercing shriek. Its great hunger and natural predatory instincts have overcome your psychic commands and, with anger blazing in its eyes, it comes lunging towards you, flailing at the air with its dagger-flints as it closes in for the kill. You step back and get ready to defend yourself as the beast rushes towards you at a breathtaking pace.

Tunnel Stalker:
COMBAT SKILL 43   ENDURANCE 48

If you win this combat, turn to **146**.

198

You hurry to the door and examine the lock. It is a unique design, quite unlike any you have seen before. It appears to be made entirely of silver with a keyhole that is smooth and circular in shape.

If you possess a Silver Rod, turn to **25**.
If you do not possess this Special Item, turn to **260**.

199

Beyond the doors you discover a large echoing hall, lit by a circle of torches which flare dimly in the moist gloom. The atmosphere is saturated with a malevolent power, an evil that is welling up from somewhere deep below ground. Immediately to your right you see a ladder which ascends to the upper floor of the tower, and to your left there is a wide staircase which leads down. Your senses scream a warning as you approach this staircase and begin to descend, but this time you choose to ignore your trusty instincts. The aura of evil which pervades this place has its source, and you are certain that it is the Doomstone of Darke, the very object you have sworn to destroy.

The staircase leads down to a winding torchlit hallway which passes through a series of narrow chambers, all empty and derelict. Eventually, you come to an iron portal and you stop for a few moments to examine the intricate engravings that embellish its age-blackened surface. Quickly you realize that the engravings are not mere decorations, they are part of a sophisticated combination lock which holds this door secure.

A host of writhing dragons are intertwined above a dial edged with ancient numerals. Each dragon has a number engraved upon its forehead, similar to those numbers which encircle the dial. Your senses inform you that the dragon numbers form a puzzle, and by solving this puzzle you will discover the "key" to this

door. Then, by turning the dial to this "key" number, the lock will disengage and the door will open.

> Study the puzzle. When you think you have found the answer, turn to the entry in this book which is the same as your answer.
> If you discover that your answer is wrong, or if you cannot solve the puzzle, turn instead to **64**.

200

The driver shouts a rude greeting to the guards at the main gates and they pull them open, allowing the cart to pass through into the town unchallenged. You stay hidden beneath the straw until the cart slows to a halt, then, very carefully, you raise your head and take a look around. You have stopped in a muddy alley which runs between a stables and an armoury. This alley opens on to a central square that has been turned into a prisoner of war compound. It is enclosed by a crude fence of wire and sharpened stakes, and is patrolled by sentries with Akataz war-dogs. You estimate at least two hundred Lencians are being held captive here, and in conditions that are shocking to behold. The men are being kept out in the open, without shelter or heat of any kind, and judging by their physical state, it looks as if the Drakkarim are purposefully starving them to death.

Shock soon turns to anger and you vow that you will do whatever you can to save these prisoners. Unseen, you slip from the rear of the cart and wait in the shadows until the chance comes for you to approach the fence and make contact with the Lencians.

Turn to **136**.

201

If you have reached the rank of Kai Grand Guardian, or higher, turn to **118**.
If you have yet to reach this level of Kai Grand Mastership, turn to **185**.

202

At first the ascent is easy, but as you approach the ledge you find that the chasm wall is dry and crumbly, making it very difficult for you to find safe purchase for your toes and fingers.

Pick a number from the *Random Number Table*. If you have Grand Huntmastery, add 2 to the number you have picked. If your present Kai rank is Grand Guardian or higher, add 1.

If your total score is now *4* or less, turn to **189**.
If it is *5* or more, turn to **89**.

203

The sounds of the struggle cease abruptly and you hear gruff Drakkarim voices yelling and cursing in anger. A yellowy light flares up and grows brighter as it approaches the broken trapdoor. Then the face of a Drakkar appears, framed in the ragged hole, illuminated grotesquely by the guttering flames of a torch. The Drakkar thrusts the torch through the shattered door and peers into the cellar, his small piggy eyes probing into every corner. You keep completely still and he fails to see you lying beneath the clutter of barrels and casks.

The moment the face and the torch disappear, you prise yourself free and then scramble upon an upright barrel in order to reach the trapdoor. Prarg and the Drakkarim are no longer in the alleyway, yet, as you pull yourself through the gaping hole, you catch sight of them in the square beyond. The Drakkarim have captured Prarg; they have tied his hands and they are marching him along the west avenue towards the centre of the town, towards Magnaarn's headquarters.

Turn to **135**.

204

You land with a splash in the powdery snow and a sharp pain lances across your right shoulder blade. You have been grazed by an arrow but, fortunately, the wound is shallow: lose 3 ENDURANCE points.

Turn to **128**.

205

Having decided to follow Magnaarn's tracks, you are now faced with the unwelcome prospect of a tiring foot-slog through the Tozaz forest, unless, of course, you can find some other means of speeding your journey. Using your Kai mastery, you scan the surrounding woodland and send out a silent call for help. A few minutes pass, then a wild dog appears. He is soon joined by a handful of other creatures: a young grey-skinned boar, two feral snow-cats and an ape-like Rhudun. Unfortunately, none are large or sturdy enough to carry you any great distance.

Then, from out of the snow-laden undergrowth, bursts forth a wild stag. It is a magnificent animal, as large and as strong as any stallion. Subdued by your commands, it approaches and tilts it antlered head to allow you to climb upon its back. Obediently it responds as you steer it through forest, heading westwards in the wake of Magnaarn's troops.

Shortly after dusk you come to the banks of the River Shug, close by a small settlement of log huts which are grouped around a derelict ferry post. You dismount, and with a slap to its rump, you send the stag trotting back to its forest home. You watch him disappear towards the distant tree-line, then you turn back to the river and approach the huts on foot.

Turn to **278**.

206

The arrow hits the creature squarely in the chest but its tip fails to penetrate the bone armour. With a shriek of anger and contempt, the Ciquali knocks Prarg aside and comes lumbering towards you with both claw-tipped hands outstretched. Swiftly you shoulder your bow and unsheathe your weapon in readiness to repel this beast as it makes a desperate lunge for your throat.

Ciquali Chieftain:
COMBAT SKILL 34   ENDURANCE 32

If you win this combat, turn to **168**.

207

Suddenly a dozen razor-sharp sword blades lunge from out of the walls and come scything towards you at waist-height. You shout a warning to Prarg and push him to the floor, an action which saves his life, but in doing so it leaves you vulnerable to this trap. You try to twist aside but you are gashed across your stomach and lower back: lose 5 ENDURANCE points.

The blades retract and lock back into the walls with a deadly slickness. You staunch your bleeding wounds and, when you are sure that this trap no longer poses a threat to your lives, you stagger to your feet and move forward to take a closer look at the door.

Turn to **275.**

208

As you ride along this road of frozen earth, the sky begins to darken ominously and the weather closes in. What begins as a light flurry of snow soon deteriorates into an icy squall which cuts through you like a knife. Your Magnakai skills protect you from the cold, but Captain Prarg is not so fortunate. He utters not a word of complaint but you can sense that he is in great discomfort. Moreover, your horse, already tired from the exertions of the escape, is greatly weakened by the icy winds. Eventually it can carry you no further and you are forced to halt and dismount.

Your Kai senses warn you that enemy cavalry are in pursuit. You are a few miles ahead of them but their mounts are fresh and the distance between you is shrinking rapidly. You are about to suggest to Prarg that you abandon the horse altogether and seek shelter in the surrounding forest, when suddenly there is a lull in the storm and the falling snow thins out to reveal an unexpected sight.

You have stopped near the crest of a hill. Below you the forest road descends to a stone bridge which crosses a frozen stream. A rough log cabin stands beside this bridge, and a thin trail of woodsmoke rises from its crooked chimney indicating that it is occupied. At the rear you see stables and at once you sense the presence of horses.

If you wish to approach the cabin and attempt to take a fresh mount from the stables, turn to **47**.

If you choose to abandon your exhausted horse and take to the forest on foot, turn to **287**.

209

You steer the boat towards the river bank and as soon as the prow embeds itself in the mud, you disembark and make your way quickly towards two lines of ramshakle huts which are standing near the water's edge. A narrow alley separates these hovels, and it is from here that you observe the town's defences and try to assess how many Drakkarim are stationed within this stronghold.

The town itself comprises a sorry collection of battle-damaged buildings, ringed by a perimeter wall of logs which is shored up in many places. Several long and bitter battles have been fought here over the past year, and everywhere you look the vivid scars of war are plain to see. The town is strangely quiet and it appears to be weakly protected. The Drakkarim garrison are few in number, and those that you have seen so far appear to be either young, old, or walking wounded.

Night is beginning to draw in. The Drakkarim are lighting the torches which line the perimeter wall, and a change of guard is taking place at the main gate. You are considering leaving this town and continuing on your way towards Darke, when suddenly you see something which makes you change your mind.

Turn to **46**.

210

You utter the words of the Brotherhood spell "Silence" and within the confines of the cabin all sound ceases. The Drakkarim sergeant screams for help, but to his amazement, he finds he has suddenly been struck dumb. You unsheathe your weapon and rush forward to strike him down, determined to finish him before the effects of the spell wear off.

Drakkarim Sergeant:
COMBAT SKILL 30   ENDURANCE 29

Due to the surprise of your spell and the speed of your attack, ignore any ENDURANCE loss you may sustain in the first round of this combat.

If you win the combat, turn to **48**.

211

Fearful of what may happen if your stay in this chamber any longer, you retrace your steps and make your way swiftly to the place where you first emerged from the collapsed passage. You pause here to catch your breath, then you continue along the tunnel until, once more, you find yourself standing at the edge of the chasm. You scan this vast and dismal fissure, hoping to find a means of escape from this grim subterranean prison.

If you possess Kai-alchemy, turn to **305**.
If you do not possess this Discipline, turn to **125**.

212

An ominous noise comes rolling across the plain from the city of Darke, a thunderous boom that shakes the very ground on which you lie. You look towards the city and see that the battle is growing ever fiercer. But now there is a new and sinister aspect. Flickerings of magical fire can be seen dancing along battlements, engulfing friend and foe alike. You sense that it is the work of Magnaarn; he and his Nadziranim allies are responsible for this.

Then, through the smoke of battle, you see a Lencian flag flying proudly amidst the carnage that is taking place on the coastal plain to the south of the city. Here, King Sarnac's crusaders have turned an enemy flank and are storming its weakened centre. Maquin and Schera see the flag and, encouraged by the cheers of their own men, they decide to march at once in support of the crusader's brave attack.

You wish them both good fortune, for you know the time has come to part company with these brave men. Their destiny awaits them on the field of battle; yours will be found inside the city of Darke itself where, if you are to fulfil your quest, you must confront Warlord Magnaarn.

You bid them farewell and watch as they lead their men in a marching column along the river road towards the field of battle. When they are a mile distant, you set off alone across the plain towards the hamlet, which lies en route to the gates of Darke.

Turn to **140**.

213

The boat glides silently through the dark, syrupy water and within minutes the huts are lost to sight. Unlike the smooth muddy banks of Dakushna's Channel, the shores of this newly-formed passage comprise a tangle of exposed roots and rotting vegetation. A foul-smelling mist clings to these torn roots, exuding a corpse-like chill that, despite your Kai skills, makes you shiver involuntarily.

You have been following this unwelcoming canal for nearly a mile when it starts to meander towards the east, and soon you are brought to a halt when an unexpected obstruction looms into view. A matted raft of floating, frost-covered weeds has become ensnared upon the right bank, partially blocking the way ahead.

You are observing the raft, looking for a way to steer around it, when suddenly your senses alert you to a hidden danger.

If you possess Kai-alchemy, turn to **95**.
If you do not possess this Grand Master Discipline, turn to **43**.

214

Captain Schera musters his men, and posts lookouts around the town wall as a precaution in case the Drakkarim return during the night with reinforcements. He then oversees the care of the sick and wounded. You are impressed by his devotion to the men under his command and, once his duties are completed, you return with him to the armoury to formulate a plan of action. It is decided that it is too dangerous to remain here and you agree that you should leave at first light. Schera says there are sufficient boats to transport everyone downriver to Darke, but there is a risk that you could run foul of Magnaarn's troops. However, he is determined to rejoin his army. If the Lencians are still resisting Magnaarn, then he reasons that the city of Darke is where the battle is most likely to be taking place.

Before you settle down to sleep, one of Schera's men brings you some food and ale: restore 3 ENDURANCE points.

To continue, turn to **21**.

215

You land with a jolt, crashing down upon a stack of ale barrels which topple and fall, pinning you beneath them: lose 3 ENDURANCE points.

Stunned by the fall, and with blood trickling into your eyes from a gash on your forehead, at first you feel totally unable to move. Then you hear sounds that immediately stir you into action. In the alleyway above, you hear the sounds of a struggle taking place: the Drakkarim have found Prarg and they are attempting to overpower him by force.

Turn to **203**.

216

You draw your weapon and attack the ice. Time is fast running out for your trapped companion; you have but a few seconds in which to reach him or he will surely drown.

Pick a number from the *Random Number Table*.

If the weapon you are using is a Special Item, add 2 to the number you have picked. If it is a Mace, a Warhammer, an Axe, or a Broadsword, add 1. If it is a Dagger, a Quarterstaff, or a Short Sword, deduct 1.

If your total score is now *4* or less, turn to **126**.
If it is *5* or more, turn to **3**.

217

Many hours pass before you regain consciousness, and although your terrible ordeal has left you physically weakened, your mind is still as sharp and resolute as ever. You are determined to find a route to the surface and continue your quest, for even though

Magnaarn now has Captain Prarg and the Doomstone of Darke, there may yet be a way you can defeat him. Before he entombed you in the passage, he admitted that you alone posed a threat to his quest for victory over Lencia. Now that he thinks you dead and buried, you feel sure you can turn this to your advantage.

You stagger to your feet and peer along the gloomy passageway in either direction, east and west. You are anxious to pursue a route that will lead you quickly to the surface, and when you detect cold, damp air wafting from the west, you hurry this way.

But you are soon disappointed. The passageway ends abruptly at the edge of a vast chasm, formed by the same destructive powers which buried you alive. At the bottom of this great fissure is a river of black water, and high above, you glimpse a few rays of winter daylight filtering through a tiny rent in the darkness. It looks so far distant that you abandon any thought of reaching it from here and return along the passageway.

A few hundred yards beyond where you emerged, you discover an octagonal chamber that is bathed by an eerie green light. This light is emitted by fungi which blanket the walls and ceiling and illuminate a strange circular door that has an octagonal lock. You have been in the chamber for no more than a few seconds when your senses detect something is wrong. Invisible fumes are rising from the fungi, which, in your weakened state, are making you feel dizzy and nauseous.

If you possess Grand Nexus, turn to **100**.
If you do not possess this skill, turn to **262**.

218

You stand directly below the shaft and focus your Kai power on the basket-sized nests that are fixed along its walls. The incessant buzzing grows steadily louder, then several lines of large wasp-like insects emerge from the nests and escape towards the sky at the top of the shaft, driven away by your mental command.

When you feel sure that the nests are empty, you reach up and take a grip of the rough brick which lines the shaft. It offers good purchase for your fingers and toes, enabling you to climb past the nests and reach the top of the shaft in a matter of minutes.

Turn to **270.**

219

You draw an arrow, then you peep around the corner and fire at the advancing Death Knight. Your shaft hits him in the middle of his chest and knocks him flat on his back. He is fatally wounded but, incredibly, he finds the strength to reach for a horn which is strung around his neck. In his dying moments he is trying to summon help.

If you wish to fire a second arrow at the Death Knight, turn to **289.**
If you do not wish to fire again, turn to **14.**

220

Your burst of psychic energy penetrates the war-dog's mind, causing it to shriek with pain and fear. Immediately the others halt in their tracks, visibly shaken by the horrible cries of their leader, but their hesitation is short-lived. Their hunger is so great that, despite the fearsome howls of their pack master, they ignore his plight and continue their advance upon you and Captain Prarg.

If you possess Kai-alchemy, and wish to use it, turn to **304.**
If you do not possess this Grand Master Discipline, or choose not to use it, turn instead to **29.**

221

At last you strike the killing bow that sends this evil amphibian spiralling down to the bottom of the frigid lake. Once free of its grip, you take hold of Prarg's tunic and pull him towards the jagged hole in the ice. Then, with great difficulty, you climb out of the water and haul your unconscious companion to safety. His skin is deep violet, he is barely breathing, and his entire body is shaking uncontrollably. Using your healing skills, you transmit some of your body warmth through your hands to his chest and face and, within a few minutes, he comes out of his state of shock as his body returns to its normal temperature. Your prompt action has saved his life, but it has also drained you of 5 ENDURANCE points.

Make the necessary adjustments to your *Action Chart* and turn to **142**.

222

You dispatch the Drakkarim with deadly precision. Then you hide their bodies in a nearby hovel, just in case their comrades should notice their absence and care enough to come looking for them. You are keen to leave this place but, before you go, you notice that one of them is wearing a hooded leather cloak which could help you get inside the town. It is big enough to hide your Kai tunic and, when pulled up, the hood hides your face completely.

Wrapped totally in this cloak, you approach the main gates. The guards are busy admitting the latest batch of prisoners and they do not give you a second glance as you stride confidently into the town. Once inside, you head towards a dark, deserted alleyway which is sandwiched between a stables and an armoury. From here you observe the compound with a growing anger and pity for those trapped inside. Stirred by their plight, you vow to help these starving men. Patiently you watch and wait for the patrols to pass, then you scurry towards the compound fence, eager to make contact with the Lencians.

Turn to **136**.

223

Bravely the horse attempts to clear the trench but it is simply too weak. Its rear legs buckle as it tries to jump and you and Prarg are both thrown head-first into the trench. Painfully you land amongst a heap of picks, shovels, and other entrenching tools: lose 3 ENDURANCE points.

To continue, turn to **250**.

224

You empty the dead Drakkar's pockets and pouches, and discover the following items:

Dagger
Sword
Bottle (empty)
Bow
2 Arrows
Ball of String
40 Kika (equivalent to 4 Gold Crowns)

You are about to abandon the body when suddenly you notice something gleaming in the top of its left boot. It is a rod of silver, plain and unmarked, and little more than four inches in length. If you wish to keep this Silver Rod, mark it on your *Action Chart* as a Special Item which you carry in your pocket.

Satisfied that you have overlooked nothing of worth, you turn your attention to clearing the rockfall which is blocking your escape from this landing.

To continue, turn to **311**.

225

The order goes out to advance quickly towards the distant hamlet. But you have covered barely a quarter of a mile when you see enemy horsemen fast approaching from the north. Mindful of the danger of being caught out here in the open, Baron Maquin orders his mercenaries to form into a square in readiness to repel a cavalry attack. Captain Schera issues the same order to his men, and together they create a square that is bristling with spears.

The cavalry thunder towards you, undaunted by the sight of this porcupine-like defence. The first wave of Drakkarim cavalry slam against the square and are repulsed with heavy losses, then a second line hits home and it, too, fails to break through. The wounded are dragged to the centre of the square and the ranks close in readiness to face the next charge. Twice the Drakkarim have been repulsed but they are a determined enemy and they are getting ready to attack again. This time the charge is led by armoured Zagganozod, on warhorses that are sheathed with plates of bronze. Their armour, and the sheer weight of their attack, smashes a corner of the square and, in a terrible moment of carnage and chaos, several enemy horsemen break into the middle of the square and trample the helpless wounded.

You rush to help them but, in the heat of the battle, you are knocked down by a riderless horse. Before you can get to your feet you are attacked simultaneously by two enemy lancers, who are maniacally determined to pin you to the ground with their lances.

2 Zagganozod Lancers:
COMBAT SKILL 36   ENDURANCE 43

If you win this combat, turn to **86**.

226

The sound of a dog growling loudly in your ear stirs you to sudden wakefulness. Instinctively you reach for your weapon, but as you do so, a set of sharp fangs closes about your wrist: lose 2 ENDURANCE points.

Fiercely you struggle to free yourself from the vice-tight jaws of an Akataz. The war-dog hangs on to your wrist with grim determination until a blow to its neck with the edge of your left hand kills it instantly. As its body drops to the snow, you unsheathe your weapon and call out to Prarg. He replies, but his voice is distant and filled with desperation. You climb the river bank, cursing yourself for allowing your guide to take the first watch. Overcome by fatigue he must have fallen asleep, allowing a pack of marauding Akataz to fall upon you without warning.

As you crest the bank, you see Prarg stabbing and slashing with his sword, fighting like a wild man to save himself from a dozen of the snapping, snarling war-dogs.

"Quickly, Prarg!" you shout, as you rush to his aid, "Stand back-to-back. Don't let them separate us or you're done for!"

Wild Akataz Pack:
COMBAT SKILL 40   ENDURANCE 55

These war-dogs are especially susceptible to psychic attack. Double all bonuses you would normally receive should you decide to use a psychic attack during this combat.

If you win the combat, turn to **160**.

227

It is late afternoon when you catch sight of a town on the horizon. You check your map and discover it to be Konozod, a fortified Drakkarim stronghold. As the river carries you closer, you magnify your vision and see that it is built upon the left bank of the Shug. A huge stone bridge spans the river, and beneath this you see that the waterway is blocked by a barrier of chained logs.

If you wish to allow your boat to drift towards this barrier, turn to **282**.

If you decide to avoid the barrier, you can put ashore and continue on foot by turning to **209**.

228

You get to your feet and hurry along this tunnel in the opposite direction. Before long you find yourself in a section of this underground labyrinth which has suffered greatly during the recent rockfalls. Many fissures have opened up the stone floor and shattered the walls, but you take these obstacles in your stride and soon arrive at a ruined staircase which ascends to a landing. Here you are confronted by the corpse of a Drakkarim guard. It is slumped beside a mound of rubble which is blocking the stairs to the next level above. A quick examination of the dead body reveals that both arms are broken. Injured and trapped here by the rockfall, it appears that this guard eventually died of thirst.

If you wish to search the body further, turn to **224**.

If you wish to attempt to clear away the rubble that is blocking the stairs, turn to **311**.

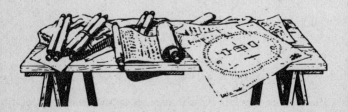

229

Immediately below the window of the grain tower sits a Drakkar lancer astride his warhorse. He is one of a dozen troopers who

have been posted around the perimeter of the square to guard its many exits, but he is more interested in watching the execution than carrying out his duty. His lance is sheathed in a tube-like scabbard fixed to the rear of his saddle, and all his attention is focused on the platform. He is unaware that you are hiding barely a few yards from where he sits.

The officer puts away his oiled stone and a murmur of expectation ripples through the assembled Drakkarim as he gets ready to raise the axe. Captain Prarg has no more than a few minutes left to live; you must act now if you are to save him. Quickly, you climb through the open window and leap from the ledge on to the back of the unwary lancer below.

Pick a number from the *Random Number Table*. If you possess Grand Huntmastery, add 3 to the number you have picked.

If your total score is now *0–8,* turn to **45**.
If your total score is now *9* or more, turn to **156**.

230

As one, the soldiers draw their weapons and come rushing towards the ground floor entrance to the tower. You retreat from the window and look around for a means of escape for already you can hear the first of the enemy climbing the stairs. With fear running cold in your veins you cross to a window on the far side of the tower. But before you reach it you are confronted at the top of the stairs by two formidable warriors. They are Death Knights, the fighting elite of the Drakkarim.

Death Knights:
COMBAT SKILL 38   ENDURANCE 40

If you win this combat in three rounds or less, turn to **32**.
If this combat takes four rounds or longer to resolve, turn instead to **144**.

231

The bolt enters the keyhole and shatters the lock with a deafening boom. The heavy door is flung open, and you see standing before you two Tukodak guards, both visibly shaking from the effects of concussion. Before they come to their senses and reach for their weapons, you rush forward and silence them both with two swift and deadly open-handed blows to their necks.

Turn to **76.**

232

You pause to incant the words of the Brotherhood spell "Strength" and within seconds you feel the fatigue disappear from your aching muscles. A vibrant sense of power and well-being infuses your whole body, enabling you to attack the rockfall with increased effect. Soon you have removed enough debris to enable you to squeeze through the gap to a clear section of the stairwell beyond. Once here, you block the opening behind you, and then race up the steps to the level above.

Turn to **159.**

233

You rise at dawn and peer out of the cabin porthole to be greeted by a wondrous sight, for the *Skyrider* is now flying west along the Tentarias, the great divide that parts the two continents of Magnamund. You are soaring more than a mile above blue-green waters which shimmer in the early morning sun. Sunlight is also reflecting from the snow-capped mountain peaks of the Great Bor and Boradon mountains which rise up on either side to form a gigantic corridor of unyielding stone. Fondly the crew cast their eyes across the northern landscape, for this is the magnificent realm of Bor, the place of their birth, and many years have elapsed since they last visited their native land.

The weather remains clear and swift progress is made as the *Skyrider* follows its course along the Tentarias towards the Gulf of Lencia. By mid-morning you pass within a few miles of Humbold, capital of Eru, then emerge from the mountain corridor to a less-enchanting sight. To the north, as far as the eye can see, stretches a dull and sickly mire. It is the infamous Hellswamp, an infernal morass of twisted vegetation and treacherous, shifting mudflats. Slowly the hours pass and the anticipation of your arrival at Vadera steadily grows. Then, at two hours past noon, the lookout catches first sight of the city-port nestling in its protected bay along the Lencian coast. You join Nolrim at the prow as skilfully he begins a descent towards the main square, the only place large enough to accommodate the craft in the closely packed quarters of this populous city.

At first, the sight of the *Skyrider* gliding towards their city causes a wave of panic among the Vaderans, who mistake it for a Drakkarim machine of war. But this initial fear is soon assuaged when the tower lookouts pass word that your mast bears a Sommlending flag. Upon landing, masses of curious citizens surge from out of the surrounding streets to form a ring of bodies around the airship's keel. Then a troop of armoured guardsmen push through the crowds and the air is filled with the buzz of their excited speculation. After a brief consultation with Lord Floras, they escort you both to the Vadera Citadel for an immediate audience with King Sarnac.

Turn to **23.**

234

Unexpectedly your arrow pierces the creature's heart, which is located at its midriff, and brings the beast crashing on to the snow. For a few moments it twitches and shivers fitfully, then it stiffens and lies still with a sudden abruptness. Prarg regains his composure and sheepishly he steps forward to look at the dead creature.

"The Gods are watching over us, Sire," he says, quite respectfully. "This beast is a Mawtaw. Few can say they have defeated this fearsome king of the Tozaz forest."

You decide to press on without delay, just in case there are others of its breed close by. Your instinct and pathsmanship skills lead you in a northerly direction and you cover more than five miles before the trees begin to thin out. Then you emerge from the forest to be greeted by an unexpected and spectacular sight.

Turn to **174.**

235

The two escorts enter the alleyway and, although you are less than ten feet away from them, they fail to see you hiding in the shadowy doorway. You watch as they open the sack and proceed to pick over and divide its contents. It is filled with the spoils of battle: items of value which they have taken from prisoners or stolen from the dead.

They laugh greedily until they hear the gruff shouts of their sergeant who is standing at the main gates, shouting out their names. Quickly they hide their booty in a hole beneath an empty horse trough, then they leave the alleyway and hurry back to the town.

If you wish to uncover the hiding place and search the sack, turn to **290**.

If you choose instead to follow these two Drakkarim, turn to **124**.

236

The dark alleys and streets surrounding the gaol are illuminated by a hundred guttering brands. Magnaarn's soldiers are everywhere, casting their suspicious eyes over every section of the nighted town laid bare by their torches. Your Kai skills keep you hidden from sight and soon you reach the gaol, but only to discover that the entrance is now heavily guarded by a platoon of Drakkarim.

You abandon your hopes of entering by the front door and instead you circle around to an alley at the rear of the building where you discover a line of windows, each one criss-crossed with iron bars. Instinct leads you to the last in the line and you peer inside to see Captain Prarg lying on a bed of filthy straw. He looks in poor shape; both his eyes are bruised, his lips are swollen, and his bushy moustache is caked with dried blood. You whisper his name and wearily he turns his head towards the cell window. Then he sees you and suddenly his whole face lights up with renewed hope.

"Thank the Gods you are still free, Lone Wolf," he says quietly, pressing his battered face to the bars. "The Drakkarim have tried to make me talk but I have kept silent. They know nothing about the mission."

You examine the cell window and reassure Prarg that you will soon spring him from this gaol, but he insists that you do not risk your life on his account.

"Listen, Sire. I have learned that Magnaarn isn't here in Shugkona. When the gaolers beat me, I feigned unconsciousness and overheard them say that their leader is at a place called Antah. It's a ruined temple some forty miles away to the north. They talked of certain victory now that their warlord has found 'the stone.' Please, Lone Wolf, I beseech you to continue without me. Go to Antah and defeat Magnaarn, before it is too late."

Then a yellowy flicker of torchlight at the end of the alley cuts short your conversation. It is a Drakkarim patrol. They turn the corner and come marching towards you with purposeful steps.

"Don't give up hope, Captain," you say, as you make ready to run from the approaching patrol, "I'll come back for you."

Turn to **72.**

237
You have covered no more than a few hundred yards of this dark and dreary tunnel when you sense imminent danger. You stop and, using your Kai tracking skills, you attempt to identify the nature of this threat.

If you possess Grand Pathsmanship, turn to **44.**
If you do not possess this Discipline, turn to **301.**

238
You send one of the scouts to summon Captain Schera and his men, and when they arrive they are treated most hospitably by the mercenaries who, despite their own hunger, unselfishly share out their meagre rations.

You stay here overnight and break camp at dawn. The Baron's regiment has suffered heavily in battle and now totals little more than forty men, and so you have no difficulty in finding room for them in the boats. Captain Schera is especially pleased to have these warriors aboard. Despite their losses, they are a cheerful group and they help lift the morale of his men.

The journey downstream passes swiftly and without incident until, shortly before noon, the sky grows steadily darker. An orange glow illuminates the distant horizon, and you can see many pinpoints of fire spread all across the land. An eerie silence descends on the flotilla as it draws nearer to the city of Darke. Shortly after, you see lines of troops marching towards the glowing skyline. Then you witness isolated actions taking place in the surrounding fields as groups of Lencian knights, cut off during the retreat, fight desperate hand-to-hand battles with Drakkarim cavalry. Some Drakkarim horse scouts have reached the river bank and, as you pass them, they open fire at you with their bows. But the swift current soon carries the flotilla away and there are few casualties.

It is an hour past noon when you first see the forbidding city of Darke. A great battle is raging around its mighty walls and bastions, and the noise and stench of this fierce conflict comes gusting towards you on the chill winter wind. The river current is getting stronger as it approaches the sea, and so you signal to the other boats to row for the bank. You put ashore on the right bank and both Captain Schera and Baron Maquin have their men take up defensive positions here. There is a road close by, running parallel to the river, and beyond it lies a snowy expanse of open plain on which many regiments of Drakkarim, and some Giaks, are marching towards the city. You are observing the distant battle when a large black carrion crow lands on a nearby log and stares at you with a cold, beady eye.

If you possess Animal Mastery, turn to **152**.
If you do not possess this Discipline, turn to **271**.

239

You peer through the grimy glass and see a grizzled old Drakkar sitting in front of a blazing fire. A briar pipe hangs precariously from the corner of his bearded mouth and he puffs fitfully at its contents as he reads from a tattered, leather-bound book which lies open in his lap.

You sense that he is a veteran of many battles who, now that he is too old to fight, has been given the undemanding task of guarding this river crossing. Mindful that time is fast running out, you leave the window and hurry on towards the stables.

Turn to **106**.

240

You settle yourself close to the lock which holds the portal secure and, using your Discipline, you cause the ancient mechanism to vibrate. The portal begins to resonate and hairline cracks appear in the stone surrounding the lock. Then there is a loud bang; the lock has disintegrated.

Confidently you move forward and place your shoulder to the portal. One hard push is all that is needed to break the seal of dirt, and slowly it creaks open.

Turn to **10**.

241

You ease open the window and climb in, making an agile and silent entry. The Drakkarim sergeant, who is pilfering his Captain's private stock of wine, belches loudly, then tilts the bottle back to take another long gulp. He is unaware of you moving towards his back, and does not feel the blow to his neck that is to seal his doom.

The Drakkar shudders and, with an open-mouthed look of surprise, closes his eyes and drops lifelessly to the floor. Quickly you step over his body and hurry to the table to study the map. To your disappointment, the map turns out to be merely a construction plan of the encampment. If offers no clues to Magnaarn's present location.

If you wish to search this cabin more thoroughly, turn to **9**.
If you choose to leave the cabin and return to Prarg, turn to **251**.

242

You watch as the cavalry steadily approaches. As they come closer you recognize them to be Zagganozod, a unit of armoured Drakkarim troopers of a type you once encountered many years ago, during a quest that took you to the land of Eru. The enemy horsemen reach the road and you can tell by their gait that they are battle-weary.

"Prepare!" says Schera, and his whispered command is passed all along the line.

The enemy cross the road and draw closer; they intend to water their horses at the river. They are less than ten yards distant when Baron Maquin yells the order to attack and, as one, the combined force of Lencians and League-landers rise up from hiding and catch the Drakkarim totally by surprise.

Turn to **49**.

243

You are nearing the base of the stone ramp when suddenly you are seen by one of the Tukodak guards. He grunts a warning to his comrade. Quickly you draw your weapon in readiness to meet them as, shoulder to shoulder, they level their spears and move down the ramp towards you.

Tukodaks: COMBAT SKILL 38   ENDURANCE 34

If you win this combat, turn to **279**.

244

You take an arrow from your quiver and place it to your bow in readiness to shoot. You gauge the range at forty yards as you take aim at the Drakkar officer. Patiently you wait for him to reach the execution block and, at the very moment he stops moving, you release your straining bowstring and send your arrow arching through the air towards his head.

Pick a number from the *Random Number Table*. If you have Grand Weaponmastery with Bow, add *3* to the number you have picked.

If your total score is 5 or less, turn to **166**.
If it is 6 or more, turn to **182**.

245

The creature opens its great jaws and from the depths of its throat it coughs forth a guttering ball of flame. Immediately, your senses alert you to the fact that this is no ordinary fireball; it is wholly psychic in nature. It comes roaring towards you like a mini-sun trailing fiery orange sparks. You strike at it with the Sommerswerd, and as your divine blade connects, the fiery ball suddenly explodes into a million motes of light which rapidly dissolve.

The sudden jolt of contact knocks you backwards. Before you fully recover your footing, the creature seizes its advantage and comes leaping through the air towards your chest.

Turn to **255**.

246

The misguided knight falls unconscious at your feet. Before he recovers, you take to your heels and continue on across the plain which leads inexorably towards the gates of Darke.

As you approach the city, the din of battle fills your ears. The shouts of angry men, the neighs of galloping steeds, the clang of riven steel and the terrible screams of the slain buffet you remorselessly. Then, all of a sudden, you are plunged into the battle and to survive you are forced to cleave your way through a seemingly endless wall of enemy troops. It is as if they are gladly willing to sacrifice themselves in order to prevent you from reaching the apex of the slope that ascends to the shattered gates of the city. Undeterred, you forge a bloody path through this Drakkarim horde, wielding your weapon with deadly precision, every blow claiming an enemy soul. It is not until you are standing upon the very threshold of the gates that you encounter more formidable defenders. The breached gates are being held by a trio of blood-spattered Tukodaks. They are in a state of battle-frenzy which you sense has been magically induced. Wild-eyed with savage blood-lust, they scream maniacally as they rush at you with their bloodied blades.

The breached gates are held by a trio of blood-
spattered Tukodaks who rush at you with bloodied blades.

"For Sommerlund!" you cry, as you steel yourself to meet their attack.

3 Tukodak Guardians (in battle frenzy):
COMBAT SKILL 44   ENDURANCE 44

If you win this combat, turn to **116**.

247

Shortly you reach a small secluded cove where Captain Prarg discovers a rusty anchor. It is a landmark, left on purpose by agents of King Sarnac to point the way to the cave where they have left your boat and provisions. You find the cave and together you haul the boat down the beach and raise its coal-black sail before pushing it out into the icy waters of the Tentarias.

Once aboard, you trim the sail whilst Prarg takes charge of the rudder. There is a good wind and within minutes your tiny craft is bobbing towards the far western channel of the Hellswamp, twenty miles distant. You ask Prarg if this dark estuary has a name, and he replies, "Yes. The Drakkarim call it 'Dakushna's Channel' after the Darklord who once commanded the city-fortress of Kagorst. They say it is a fitting dedication, for the waterway is as deadly and as treacherous as the being after whom it is named."

Turn to **55**.

248

You follow the tunnel for a mile further until it opens into a vast underground cistern. Slimy water splashes down the slick sides of this vertical shaft to mix with the rushing river before disappearing into a whirlpool which is swirling at its centre. The noise here is almost unbearable and you look around for some means of escape. The walkway ends at a rusty iron ladder which is cemented into the wall and ascends the shaft for as far as you can see. Slowly you climb this ladder, testing every rung carefully before trusting it to your weight.

You climb for an hour before reaching the entrance to a man-sized tunnel set into the wall of the shaft. Here you leave the ladder and follow this damp passageway until you come to a small, smooth-walled chamber. At first it appears to be raining, then you notice that the ceiling is badly broken and water is dripping constantly from the cracks. Opposite the tunnel exit there is a stone door. Anxious to escape, you hurry across the chamber and place your shoulder to this heavy portal in an attempt to force it open, but unfortunately it is locked. Then you detect something unusual, an acrid burning smell. Your heart skips a beat when suddenly you realize that your cloak and tunic are smouldering and giving off wisps of bluish smoke. The fluid raining from the ceiling is not water at all—it is corrosive acid!

If you possess Magi-magic, and wish to use it, turn to **130**.

If you possess Grand Nexus, and wish to use it, turn to **240**.

If you do not possess any of these Disciplines, or choose not to use them, turn instead to **184**.

You brief the three Lencians to spread out into an extended line and to watch carefully for your signals before you scale the river bank and make your approach to the trees. They all seem to be competent scouts but you have your reservations. Had it not been for Schera's insistence, you would have preferred to have reconnoitred this copse alone.

Silently you creep forward through the snow, using the sparse undergrowth to your advantage wherever possible. You are less than a hundred yards into the copse when you spy a small cabin hidden among the trees. It comprises four white canvas tents attended by a dozen lean and hungry-looking human soldiers armed with longbows. A furled battle-flag stands propped against one of the tents and you signal to your nearest scout to join you, hoping he will be able to identify its chequered black-and-white design.

"They're League-landers of Ilion," whispers the scout, staring at the campsite. "I know that flag well. They're good mercenaries, these men, loyal to the King. We fought alongside them at Hokidat."

You are anxious about going forward and making contact with the mercenaries. If they are as good as your scout claims, there is a real danger that they will fire first and ask questions later. You tell your companion of your fears and he smiles.

"Don't worry, Sire," he says, "I know how to contact them."

Turn to **284.**

250

You scramble to your feet to see that your horse is still close by. He is standing at the forest's edge, steam rising from his flanks as hungrily he swallows mouthfuls of snow to cool himself down. You call to the animal, using your Magnakai skills, and at once he responds obediently to your silent commands. Drakkarim archers are now running from the outer defences and you are in danger of being surrounded unless you can make a speedy escape. You and Prarg remount the horse and set off at a gallop along the forest's edge. Only when you are safely beyond the range of the enemy's bows do you rejoin the road and head off towards the north.

Turn to **208.**

251

As you are about to leave the cabin, you notice a lantern hanging on a hook beside the door. You take it down, flip up its glass cover, then cast it into the corner where it immediately sets fire to a heap of clothes. The fire will cover your tracks and, hopefully, cause enough of a diversion to enable you to escape from the encampment unchallenged.

As you hoped, the fire spreads quickly and, as you sprint across the frozen ground towards the forest's edge, you glance over your shoulder to see bright orange flames roaring from the open doorway, and a pall of black smoke rising into the steel-grey sky. You reach Prarg and together you hurry deeper into the forest. The fire covers your escape, but it also draws several Drakkarim patrols back to the encampment. You are forced to make a wide detour to the west in order to avoid these returning soldiers and your new route takes you across a steep and rugged part of the Tozaz forest previously unexplored by your guide.

The difficult terrain slows you down and you cover less than six miles before failing light and the increasing sightings of Drakkarim patrols force you to halt and make camp for the night. From the safety of a treetop, fifty feet above the forest floor, you rope yourself to the trunk before settling down to sleep. You are hungry and, unless you possess the Discipline of Grand Huntmastery, you must now eat a Meal or lose 3 ENDURANCE points.

To continue, turn to **81**.

252

The chilling echo of Magnaarn's voice is drowned by new sounds: the rattle of chains and the rumble of falling stone. You shout a warning to Prarg and he dives aside only just in time to avoid being crushed by a heavy portcullis. The great stone portal slams down, partitioning the passageway and separating you from the Captain. The dust has barely settled when a section of the passage wall slides open behind Prarg, and a trio of Magnaarn's Tukodak bodyguards leap out and seizes him. Your companion is unarmed and he is quickly and brutally overpowered. Anger floods your mind and you vow to get even with these cruel Drakkarim, but they are not impressed by your threat. They are aware of your exceptional skills yet they feel safe behind the portcullis. With a knife held to Prarg's throat they taunt you and dare you to retaliate.

If you have a Bow and wish to use it, turn to **154**.
If you do not, or if you choose not to use it, turn to **31**.

253

Suddenly the gentle buzzing becomes an angry drone. Then from out of the lowest nest comes a swarm of wasp-like insects, each as large as a clenched fist. Alerted by your body warmth, they hurtle down the shaft and gather in a menacing cloud around the opening. For a few moments they hover there, virtually motionless, then they begin to circle the ceiling, led by an insect whose vivid scarlet markings stand out in stark contrast to the black and yellow striped torsos of the others.

As the encircling swarm gathers speed, the lower section of their bodies begins to glow, illuminating needle-like stingers in their

From out of the lowest nest comes a swarm of wasp-like insects, each as large as a clenched fist.

tails. You draw your weapon and get ready to defend yourself lest they should attack, but you are caught off-guard when suddenly the leading insects fire their stingers at you. Diving aside, you avoid being hit by this volley of venom-tipped needles, but as you scramble to your feet the remainder of the swarm break away and dive down to attack your unprotected back.

Antah Wasps: COMBAT SKILL 40   ENDURANCE 30

These insects are immune to all psychic attacks.

If you win the combat, turn to **111**.

254

Using your pathsmanship skills, you identify and gather up a handful of edible roots, fungi and berries from the forest floor which you then offer to Prarg. At first he thinks you are joking. Then, once you assure him that they are nutritious, he accepts this dubious selection and starts to eat.

''Damn rabbit food,'' he mumbles, but you notice that he is careful not to waste a crumb. Meanwhile, you scan the surrounding forest, ever watchful for enemies. For the last hour you have had a growing suspicion that something has been watching you. Your senses detect the presence of a hostile enemy, closing from the east. Now the suspicion has become a sure belief, and the moment Prarg finishes his meal, you suggest that you be on your way as swiftly as possible.

Turn to **13**.

255

Desperately you roll across the black stone floor to avoid the creature's initial attack. Your swift reactions save you from its razor claws, but it, too, possesses lightning reflexes. It leaps once more and you barely have enough time to unsheathe your weapon before it lands upon you and slams you to the ground.

Tarhdemon (polymorphed Nadziran):
COMBAT SKILL 42   ENDURANCE 42

If you win this combat, turn to **61**.

256

Shaken but unharmed, you wade out to the boat where Prarg helps you aboard.

"That was too close for comfort," says Prarg, as he struggles to free the oars and set them in place.

"You can count yourself lucky to have escaped with your life. The first time I navigated these channels I lost three good men in a Gorodon attack. Those beasts are the bane of this accursed place . . . yet, t'is true to say, there are other creatures here that are far deadlier."

Using the oars you soon reach the west bank where, once safely ashore, you encamp on a strip of frozen loam that overlooks a bleak expanse of marsh. Night has fallen and so, too, has the temperature. From the shelter of your upturned boat you cast your experienced eye across the darkening skies and see banks of cloud, heavy with snow, scudding the distant horizon. They are an unwelcome sight, the precursors to a winter storm.

Prarg volunteers to continue the first watch but, mindful that his need for rest is greater than yours, you insist that he gets some sleep. For four hours you sit and scan the bleak horizon, your mind filled with unanswered questions about the mission and the dangers you have yet to face. While you ponder what awaits you in the near future, you remain watchful and alert, your encounter on the east bank still vivid in your mind. Fortunately, the increasing cold dissuades the Hellswamp's inhabitants from leaving their lairs this night and your watch passes without incident.

At first light you continue your long voyage north up the Gourneni River to Bear Rock. By mid-morning the snow has returned and your progress is soon hampered by a whipping wind that blows persistently in your faces. Shielded by your Magnakai skills, the sub-zero temperatures cause you little concern as you tirelessly work the oars. But Prarg is not so fortunate and, as the hours pass, the bitter cold saps his strength until he is unable to continue rowing. Single-handedly you take over at the oars while your guide, swathed in blankets, mans the rudder and acts as pilot through the narrower sections of this treacherous waterway.

Turn to **98**.

257

Rising to the top of the stairs comes a lumbering hulk with hungry, scarlet eyes. The beast is covered with a vile fur which glistens in the eerie light of the landing. Its long sinewy arms are outstretched and in both of its huge hands there are chunks of daggerlike flint. Its distended belly skims the floor as it stalks closer, and a brown gluey saliva runs freely from its fanged lower jaw. With the rockfall preventing a hasty escape, you draw your weapon and steel yourself for combat with this nightmarish creature.

Tunnel Stalker:
COMBAT SKILL 43   ENDURANCE 48

If you win this combat, turn to **82**.

258

The few war-dogs that manage to survive the combat now slink away into the forest like frightened pups. Prarg, elated by the victory, is confident that they will not be back this night. You are not so sure, and as you turn to go back to the boat to catch some sleep, you warn him to remain vigilant whilst he is on guard.

Turn to **194**.

259

You unsheathe your weapon and warn Prarg to hold tight as you bear down on a collision course with the three Drakkarim sentries.

Pick a number from the *Random Number Table*. If you possess the Discipline of Grand Weaponmastery, and have reached the Kai rank of Sun Knight, add 3 to the number you have picked.

If it is *0–8*, turn to **121**.
If it is *9* or more, turn to **57**.

260

You examine the circular lock with care and sense that it is protected by a powerful magical spell. Any attempt to pick this lock could prove fatal.

If you possess Kai-alchemy, turn to **187**.
If you do not possess this Discipline, turn to **92**.

261

The deadly bolts come screaming towards you and Captain Prarg with an unnerving accuracy that sends a cold spike of fear coursing down your spine. Impact is imminent.

If you possess Kai-alchemy *and* have reached the rank of Sun Knight, turn to **151**.
If you do not possess this Discipline, or have yet to reach this rank, turn to **300**.

262

You feel yourself awakening; all you wish for is to sleep. But your senses warn you that to fall asleep here could prove fatal. You know you must do something, and quickly, if you are to avoid unconsciousness.

If you possess some Oede or some Sabito, turn to **191**.
If you possess neither of these substances, turn to **211**.

263

The journey downstream is swift and easy. The icy river cuts a direct path across the frozen plain before it wends its way through an expanse of low, rolling hills, blackened and scarred by war. Ruined hovels smoulder on the horizon and scores of snowcovered corpses, human and otherwise, lie where they died in a running battle that has swept like wildfire across this land.

Shortly after midday, you see something in the distance that sets your nerves on edge. It is a group of figures, huddled together on the river bank. You magnify your vision and identify them to be Drakkarim, possibly deserters from Magnaarn's army, who are attempting to catch fish from the river. Rather than attract their unwanted attention, you hide in the bottom of the boat and allow the current to carry you past them.

Turn to **99**.

Baron Maquin, leader of the mercenary band, regards
you with a sceptical eye.

264

You and your scouts are taken to a lookout post on the banks of the river where you meet with Baron Maquin, the leader of this mercenary band. He is a tall man, clad from neck to toe in furs that are caked with frost. A battered silver helm hides much of his battle-scarred face, but you can see enough of his distinctly Ilionian features to know at once that he is a brave man, a man of honour. He regards you with a sceptical eye, having never before met a Sommleading lord, let alone one such as you. He questions you at length and, upon hearing your story, you sense that he is greatly impressed. In return he tells you briefly of how he and his men have come to find themselves here.

''This regiment is still loyal to King Sarnac,'' he says, proudly, ''unlike the cowardly Stornlanders. They have broken their pact and now they fight 'gainst Lencia, alongside the enemy.'' The Baron spits at the ground in a show of contempt for these treacherous regiments. ''My command has been left here to fight as a rear-guard. Our orders are to ambush any Drakkarim that may try to reach Darke by river. We believe there to be many enemy reinforcements at Konozod and our task is to prevent them from joining with Magnaarn.''

You remind the Baron that you have just come from Konozod and that it is virtually empty. There are no enemy reinforcements there. Respectfully you suggest that he and his men join with you in an attempt to reach Darke, where he could join once more with the Lencian army. He considers your suggestion and, after discussing it with his men, finally he agrees.

''But first,'' he says, as he shakes your hand in friendship, ''you must summon your men to my humble camp. It will soon be dark and it is much too dangerous to travel this river at night. You could be ambushed!''

Turn to **238**.

265

As soon as the coast is clear, you leap from the ditch and sprint through a gap in the log wall. You are within a few yards of the cabin when suddenly you see two Drakkarim on horseback come galloping along a newly-laid forest track which leads to the encampment. You are in danger of being seen by them, so the moment you reach the cabin door you thrust it open and rush in.

Your sudden entrance startles a Drakkarim sergeant who is secretly sneaking a gulp of wine from his Captain's private stock. The bristle-bearded soldier chokes on his mouthful of ruby-red claret when he hears the door open, but his fear soon turns to anger when he sees it is you, and not his commander, who is standing in the doorway. He spits out the wine and hurls the half-empty bottle at your head. You dodge this missile with ease, but it has served its purpose: it has bought the sergeant the time he needs to unsheathe his heavy-bladed sword. He sneers, and your heart skips a beat when you see him get ready to shout for help. You must silence him quickly or he will alert the entire camp to your presence.

If you possess Kai-alchemy, turn to **210**.

If you do not possess this Grand Master Discipline, turn instead to **179**.

266

Slowly you wander through the smouldering ruins but discover little that has survived the fire which, at its height, must have transformed this whole town into a blazing inferno. The charred bones and skulls of those who died in the battle are strewn everywhere, and no attempt has been made to gather and bury them. You are examining the twisted remains of an iron axe when suddenly you sense that someone is nearby. You can tell that they are weak and in pain.

Instinct leads you to the ruins of an inn, and as you enter what was once its front door, you stop to listen. You can hear someone breathing. You detect they are somewhere below ground and you call out to Captain Schera to come quickly.

"What is it?" he says, as he enters the ruined inn.

"There's someone alive here," you reply. "They're somewhere beneath the floor."

Schera helps you to lift away some charred beams and you discover a trapdoor. You pull it open and slowly descend a flight of stone steps leading down into a cold, dank cellar. The sound of breathing has stopped but your suspicions are soon confirmed. There is somebody here.

Turn to **178**.

267

The creature utters a spine-chilling shriek as it comes bounding towards you, its sword-like teeth glinting in the wintery sun. You step back and draw your weapon just in time to defend yourself as it makes its first strike.

Mawtaw: COMBAT SKILL 38   ENDURANCE 50

This creature is immune to the effects of Mindblast and Psi-surge. If you choose to use Kai-surge, add only 1 point to your COMBAT SKILL.

If you possess Kai-alchemy, and have reached the rank of Sun Knight (or higher), you may increase your COMBAT SKILL and ENDURANCE point scores by 5 each for the duration of this combat.

If you win this combat, turn to **22**.

268

"Heads!" says Prarg.

You remove your hand to reveal the citadel of Holmgard stamped on the reverse side of the coin.

"Never mind, Prarg," you say, trying hard not to sound too pleased with the way things have turned out. "The time'll soon pass. Wake me in four hours and I'll take over."

Prarg gathers his weapons and equipment and, while you are settling yourself down to sleep in the relative comfort of the boat, he climbs to the top of Bear Rock to begin his cold and lonely vigil.

Turn to **226**.

269

You search the dead guard's pockets and belt pouches, and discover the following items:

Bow
2 Arrows
Ball of String
Dagger
Sword
Bottle (empty)
40 Kika (equivalent to 4 Gold Crowns)

You are about to abandon the body when suddenly you notice something gleaming in the top of its left boot. It is a rod of silver, plain and unmarked, and little more than four inches in length. If you wish to keep this Silver Rod, mark it on your *Action Charts* as a Special Item which you carry in your pocket.

Satisfied that you have overlooked nothing of worth, you turn your attention to clearing the rockfall which is blocking your escape from this landing.

Turn to **16**.

270

From the top of the shaft you look out across the sprawling ruins of Antah. You have emerged upon the flat roof of a mouldering stone crypt situated a few hundred yards from the tower by which you first entered the subterranean temple. A chill wind howls in the surrounding trees and overhead the darkening winter sky warns that night is fast approaching.

The ruins are completely deserted. The undisturbed blanket of snow which lies thick upon the ground, hiding all tracks, sorely reminds you that fifteen precious days have elapsed since your internment. You think of Captain Prarg and wonder if he is still alive, and an empty feeling gnaws at your stomach when you pause to consider the fate which may have befallen him and his Lencian countrymen now that Magnaarn is in possession of the Doomstone. You are fearful, but you are not entirely without hope. Magnaarn believes you to be dead; it is a belief that you could use to your advantage. After all, by his own admission, did he not say that you were the only threat to his victory?

Carefully you descend from the roof of the crypt and make your way through the forest to where, two weeks earlier, Magnaarn's Tukodak guards were encamped. In this clearing there are no visible remains of their campsite, but diligently you sift through the ankle-deep snow, looking for clues to where they may have gone.

If you possess Grand Pathsmanship, turn to **157**.
If you do not possess this Discipline, turn to **288**.

271

The bird suddenly takes fright and flies away, cawing long and loud as hurriedly it disappears towards the northern horizon.

Turn to **294**.

272

Hurriedly you and Prarg fix the oars in place and row with all your strength, retracing your route all the way back to where the channel first divided. Once here, you slow your boat to a halt and take some time to reconsider your plans.

Reluctantly you decide to navigate the left channel. Rather than run the risk of making any noise, you stow the oars and allow the stinking marsh wind to propel your boat along the channel, albeit at a far slower speed. Gradually you approach the cluster of huts and, as you pass before them, you see eight dwellings, each built of mud-daubed roots and thatched with rotting vegetation. They are empty but they have not been deserted. The shoreline is littered with bones, the remnants of past meals, and nearby is a crude wooden frame on which the skins of a snake and a lizard have been stretched out to dry.

"It's a Ciquali camp," whispers Prarg nervously, his eyes scouring the surrounding waters for the slightest sign of movement. During your travels you have heard tales about the Ciquali, none of which are favourable. They are the bane of the Hellswamp—

a breed of vicious amphibians, intelligent and cunning, with a taste for human flesh that makes them especially dangerous.

"Our luck's good, Lone Wolf," says Prarg, as gradually the wind carries you beyond the huts. "The camp's empty—they must be away hunting. Perhaps it was they who were lying in wait for us along the other passage?"

As soon as you lose sight of the settlement, you hoist the sail and catch the prevailing wind which propels you northwards along Dakushna's Channel. You are hungry, and unless you possess Grand Huntmastery, you must now eat a Meal or lose 3 ENDURANCE points.

To continue, turn to **98**.

273
Your sixth sense tells you that the Green Key you have in your possession will open this door. Quickly you take it from your backpack, insert it into the lock, and twist it counter-clockwise. There is a faint click, then the door creaks open to reveal a dark and desolate chamber, its brick walls dripping with evil-smelling grey slime.

If you possess Grand Huntmastery, turn to **177**.
If you do not possess this Discipline, turn to **117**.

274
When the coast is clear, you enter the stables and set a fire in the straw loft. Then, as you are leaving, you open each of the stalls so that the horses will be able to escape once the fire has taken hold. On returning to the alleyway you run to the rear of the armoury building and locate a window through which you can force an entry. It is shuttered and barred, but aided by your inate Kai skills, you are able to break it open. Unfortunately, the noise of your forced entry alerts the two Drakkarim who are on guard inside the building and, as you are squeezing through the narrow window, they attack you with their blackbladed swords.

Armoury Guards:
COMBAT SKILL 32   ENDURANCE 40

Unless you possess the Discipline of Grand Pathsmanship, reduce your COMBAT SKILL by 3 for the first round of this combat.

If you win this combat, turn to **150**.

275

To your surprise, you discover that the door is unlocked. You push it and it swings open to reveal an empty chamber. You detect a strong presence of evil lurking somewhere nearby and you warn Prarg of what you sense. Cautiously, the two of you leave this chamber by a passage which leads to a flight of black stone steps. You ascend the steps to a domed chamber which is sheathed with dull black stone. Heavy velvet hangings of ebony hue cover most of the walls, and all of the furnishings are upholstered with the same morbid cloth. The sensation of evil is stronger here, so strong that you feel as if you are slowly suffocating.

"It's here . . ." you whisper, your hand reaching to your weapon, "the Doomstone. I can feel its presence!"

Suddenly there is a movement away to your left and a blast of white-hot energy comes roaring towards your face. You dive aside in time to avoid it, but the bolt rebounds from the steel-hard wall and glances off the back of Prarg's head, knocking him unconscious.

Turn to **145**.

276

Using the Brotherhood spell—"Sense Evil"—you scour the surrounding woodland and a powerful sensation alerts you to danger. It is not an immediate threat, yet you can feel the invisible waves of power which are radiating from its source. The power is strong, too strong to originate from Drakkarim or a hostile forest creature. You focus your senses in the direction of this power and at once you recognize its source: it is the Doomstone of Darke.

"What's wrong, Sire?" says Prarg.

"It's the Doomstone," you reply quietly. "We're close . . . I can feel it."

Turn to **41**.

277

Prarg is understandably happy to accept your offer to stand the first watch. While he settles himself down to sleep in the relative comfort of the boat, you pull your cloak about you and climb to the top of Bear Rock where you begin your lonely vigil. For hours you sit on this windswept boulder, staring out through a curtain of swirling snow at the surrounding timberline. Despite your fatigue you stay alert and your iron discipline pays off when, shortly before midnight, you sense movement at the forest's edge. Then your super-keen Kai senses detect an animal scent on the cold air which you recognize immediately: it is Akataz.

Turn to **147**.

278

The tracks end at a wooden jetty which juts precariously into the deep, fast-flowing waters of the River Shug. Carefully you examine the ground around this landing area and, aided by your exceptional tracking skills, you make two important discoveries. You deduce that Magnaarn and his troops boarded a barge here and headed downstream towards Darke. Also, you discover that this area was used as a mustering place for a second, far larger, unit of troops. Doomwolf droppings and a Giak tooth hint at the identity of these troops, but your suspicions are confirmed when you find a bronze belt buckle which is engraved with the symbol of a fortress and a full moon. It is the symbol of the old Darklord city-fortress of Kagorst. It confirms your fears that Magnaarn has at last persuaded Kagorst to join his cause.

You are tired after your long trek. Rather than attempt to go any further, you decide instead to rest here in one of the empty cabins overnight and continue your journey at dawn.

Turn to **171**.

279

You step away from the two dead Tukodaks, sheathe your weapon, then signal to Prarg that the coast is now clear. He emerges from the trees and hurries to your side. He praises your combat skill and then he helps you to hide the bodies of the two slain guards beneath some undergrowth in the surrounding ruins. Before you leave, a quick search of their packs and pockets reveals the following items:

Enough food for 1 Meal
Dagger
2 Swords
Bow
4 Arrows

If you wish to take and keep any of the above items, remember to adjust your *Action Chart* accordingly.

To enter the unguarded tower, turn to **199**.

280

You draw upon your mental powers and launch a blast of psychic energy at the three Drakkarim sentries. The effect is instantaneous. They begin to shake uncontrollably and all three drop their spears. Unable to move aside, you trample them into the ground as you gallop through the gap in the barricade and race along the road beyond. You have passed successfully through the inner defensive line, but, as Prarg quickly points out, you have yet to reach the outer defences of Shugkona.

Turn to **28**.

281

With some difficulty you climb out of the water and haul your unconscious companion to safety. His skin is deep violet, he is barely breathing, and his entire body is shaking uncontrollably. Using your healing skills, you transmit some of your body warmth through your hands to his chest and face and, within a few minutes, he comes out of his state of shock as his body returns to its normal temperature. Your prompt action has saved his life, but it has also drained you of 5 ENDURANCE points.

Make the necessary adjustments to your *Action Chart* and turn to **142**.

As the current carries you towards the stone bridge, you row against the river's flow in order to slow your final approach to the log barrier. There are Drakkarim on the bridge and the noise of a hard collision would be sure to attract their unwanted attention. The prow grazes the muddy river bank, slowing you further, then the boat comes to an abrupt halt as it bumps against the barrier. Quickly, you leap on to the line of logs and make your way towards the bank as swiftly as the treacherously icy surface will allow.

A rickety flight of wooden steps ascends from the river to the top of the bridge. You climb them, then you crouch down and take cover behind the stone parapet. From here you observe the town's defences and try to assess how many Drakkarim are stationed within this stronghold. The town itself comprises a sorry collection of battle-damaged buildings, ringed by a perimeter wall of logs which is shored up in many places. Several long and bitter battles have been fought here over the past year, and everywhere you look the vivid scars of war are plain to see.

A rutted road crosses the bridge and leads directly to the town gates. You observe Drakkarim on guard at the bridge, and at the gate, yet you sense something is wrong. The town is strangely quiet and it appears to be weakly protected; the Drakkarim garrison is few in number, and those that you have seen so far appear to be either young, old, or walking wounded.

Night is beginning to draw in. The Drakkarim are lighting the torches which line the perimeter wall, and a change of guard is taking place at the main gate. A wagon laden with straw crosses the bridge and pulls to a halt nearby. Wearily the driver gets down from his seat, curses his aching back, then wanders off towards a nearby hovel, one of barely a dozen that are still standing outside the town's wall. While he is gone, you take the opportunity to climb into the cart and hide yourself beneath the foul-smelling straw. Soon you hear the driver's gruff voice and you feel the cart sway as he climbs back into his seat. There is the crack of a whip and, with a jolt, the cart trundles off towards the main gates.

Turn to **200**.

283

Through the open archway comes a Lencian soldier attired in the parade tunic and breeches of a Court Captain. He is unusually tall, but his most striking feature is his close-set eyes which are bright above his thin, hawk-like nose and bushy black moustache. At once you recognize this officer, for he is Captain Prarg. During the fighting at Cetza you and he led Prince Graygor's reserves in a decisive action that helped save the Eruan Guards and turn the tide of the battle in your favour.

"Well met, Sire!" he says, with a smile, "'Tis an honour to have been chosen to guide you on your noble quest."

Turn to **73**.

284

The scout places two fingers to his lips and gives a long, warbling whistle. The sound makes the mercenaries turn and stare in your direction, and you hear one of them whistle twice in reply. Your scout then calls out a request that you be allowed to enter their camp. There is a long pause, then a heavily-accented voice replies:

"Show yourselves."

Relief that you are human, and not Drakkarim, is displayed clearly on the faces of these League-landers when the four of you stand up and walk towards their camp. You receive a warm welcome from these soldiers of fortune and two of them offer to escort you to their leader—Baron Maquin.

Turn to **264**.

285

You abandon the shelter of the bridge and work your way slowly along the ice-filled ditch to a point directly in front of the tower. Here you settle to observe the Drakkarim guards who are dutifully keeping watch over the eastern approaches to the town. All you can see of them is their brutal faces peering out of the horizontal slit which runs the full circumference of the tower. After a while, three of the four Drakkarim leave the tower by a staircase at the side. Only one remains, and you decide that now would be the best time to make your move, before the three return or before their replacements show up for duty.

Prarg insists that he go first; he has crossed here once before and he knows a safe way through. The ground looks clear but there are concealed pits out there just waiting to snare the careless or unwary. You nod your agreement and, as soon as the guard turns his face away from the observation slit, Prarg makes his run. Crouching low, he half-runs, half-scampers across the clearing, keeping low and zig-zagging as he weaves a safe path through the pits. It takes him thirty seconds to reach the base of the tower, then he slips around the side and takes cover beneath the steps before beckoning you to follow.

You take a deep breath then launch yourself out into the open. With heart pounding you run towards the tower, following in Prarg's footsteps which are clearly visible in the snow. You are halfway across when suddenly the guard's face reappears at the observation slit. You pray your camouflage skills will keep you hidden for a few seconds longer, but then you see something that shakes your confidence. The guard raises a curious square of glass in front of his eyes, and at once you sense it possesses magical properties.

Pick a number from the *Random Number Table*. If you have Grand Huntmastery and you have reached the rank of Kai Grand Guardian or higher, add 1 to the number you have chosen. If you have the Discipline of Assimilance, add 2.

If it is *0–6*, turn to **62**.
If it is *7* or higher, turn to **68**.

286

From out of the grey-green gloom comes a lumbering hulk that fixes you with its hungry scarlet eyes. The beast is covered with a vile fur which glistens in the eerie light of the tunnel. Its long sinewy arms are outstretched and in both of its huge hands there are chunks of dagger-like flint. Its distended belly skims the walkway as it stalks closer, and a brown gluey saliva runs freely from its fanged lower jaw. With the grill at your back preventing your escape, you draw your weapon and get ready to defend yourself from this nightmarish creature.

Tunnel Stalker:
COMBAT SKILL 43   ENDURANCE 48

If you win this combat, turn to **146**.

287
Using your Magnakai skills you command your tired horse to descend the hill and cross the bridge. Hopefully its tracks will lead your pursuers in the wrong direction and enable you to get away. As the horse wanders off, you beckon Prarg to follow you into the dense forest. Your instincts and pathsmanship skills set you on a north-westerly tack, the direction you hope will lead eventually to Magnaarn and the hidden Temple of Antah.

You have covered two miles when suddenly you hear a sound which stops you both dead in your tracks. It is a terrible, bestial growl.

"There!" gasps Prarg, and you spin round to see a terrifying creature come slinking from out of the undergrowth.

Turn to **18**.

288
The site has been expertly cleared and very little evidence remains that Magnaarn and his bodyguard were here, yet you do manage to uncover some tracks frozen beneath the snow. They were made by men and horses, and are a little over a week old. Satisfied with your discovery, you leave the campsite and follow the tracks westward.

If you possess Animal Mastery, and have reached the rank of Kai Grand Guardian (or higher), turn to **205**.
If you do not possess this Discipline, or have yet to reach this level of Kai training, turn instead to **120**.

289
Your second arrow kills the Death Knight instantly. You shoulder your bow and run down the corridor, with Prarg close on your heels, and soon you reach a junction where you are forced to choose a direction, left or right. You call upon your Kai skills

and immediately you sense a strong presence of evil lurking at the end of the right-hand passage. You focus on the source of this evil and determine that it is the Doomstone. You tell Prarg and together you advance along the passage until you reach a closed door.

If you possess Grand Huntmastery or Grand Pathsmanship, turn to **193**.

If you possess neither of these Disciplines, turn to **207**.

290

You uncover the sack and sift through its contents. Gleaming in the dim light you see a mass of coins, silver plates and candlesticks, jewellery and all manner of precious and semi-precious stones. There are countless gold teeth, pulled no doubt from the mouths of fallen Lencian knights, and scores of trinkets and other momentoes taken from less-noble corpses. One item you sense possesses magical properties. You pull it out and, on closer inspection, you discover it to be a polished jadin amulet which is fixed to a gold neckchain.

If you decide to keep this Jadin Amulet, record it on your *Action Chart* as a Special Item which you wear around your neck. It adds + 1 to your score should you be instructed to pick a number from the *Random Number Table* to check against normal missiles (arrows, bolts, darts, etc.).

Having replaced the sack in its hole, you draw your cloak about you and approach the main gates. The guards are busy admitting the latest batch of prisoners and, helped by your camouflage skills, they do not give you a second glance as you stride confidently into the town.

Once inside, you head towards a dark, deserted alleyway which is sandwiched between a stables and an armoury. From here you observe the compound with a growing anger and pity for those trapped inside. Stirred by their plight, you vow to help these starving men. Patiently you watch and wait for the patrols to pass, then you scurry towards the compound fence to make contact with the Lencians.

Turn to **136**.

291

You enter the warehouse through a broken window and soon find a hiding place among hundreds of rolls of canvas that are being stored on the ground floor. Periodically, Drakkarim enter and search the length and breadth of this sprawling building, but they fail to detect you.

While you are hiding from their search parties, you consider your companion's plight and grow ever more fearful for his safety. You are also very anxious that, under torture, he will reveal your identity and the reason why you have come to this town. You are determined not to allow this to happen and so, as midnight approaches, you slip away from your hiding place and make your way stealthily towards the Shugkona Gaol.

Turn to **236**.

292

"Come, Prarg," you say urgently, "we must hurry from here. I sense more traps nearby."

Obediently, the Captain follows as you make your way speedily along the passageway towards a distant torchlit chamber. Upon reaching this chamber you are brought skidding to a halt by an unexpected sight.

The room is constructed entirely of polished black rock. Revealed in the torchlight is a throne of rough-hewn marble, where rests the skeletal remains of a warrior clad in mouldering furs. Bare bone gleams dully through a clinging mass of muscle and sinew, now shrunken to an iron-hard texture, and upon its skull there is perched a helm of solid gold. Set into the face of this helm is an emerald as large as your fist.

Prarg approaches the throne, tempted by the magnificent emerald, but he halts the moment you warn him that the helm is protected by a magical trap. You sense that a powerful spell of warding encircles the throne; to touch the crown would activate the spell, thereby unleashing a blast of destructive energy. The thought of being blown to atoms serves to dampen Prarg's curiosity and sheepishly he returns to your side. You give the booby-trapped

Desperately trying to draw yourself away from the
creature's grip, you strike at the tentacles which ensnare
your legs.

throne a wide berth and leave the chamber by a smooth-walled tunnel in the far wall. But you have taken no more than a dozen steps when a chill of premonition runs like a trickle of icy cold water down your spine. You halt and reach for your weapon. Then a loud voice booms out, destroying the silence.

"Welcome, Lone Wolf. Welcome to your tomb!"

Instinctively you know that it is the voice of Warlord Magnaarn.

Turn to **252**.

293

Desperately you try to tear yourself free from the creature's grip. You draw your weapon and strike at the tentacles which ensnare your legs, but the skin which sheaths them is like iron and you can barely cause a scratch. Then you sense that the creature's most vulnerable spot is its single eye and, with renewed vigour, you dive down and attack it relentlessly.

Gartoth: COMBAT SKILL 43　　ENDURANCE 50

If you win this combat, turn to **221**.

294

Baron Maquin and Captain Schera are anxious to move their men away from the river bank. Their military training has taught them to avoid placing their troops with their backs to an impassable body of water, for if the enemy were to attack, there would be no way to escape. You understand their concern and, using your ability to magnify your vision, you scan the landscape in search of a more advantageous position. A mile away, to the north-west, you see a tiny hamlet. It appears to be deserted and you suggest to the two officers that they move their men there. Briefly they discuss your suggestion and both agree that it would be a safer position.

The order to move is passed along the ranks and the men prepare to leave the boats and go forward. You take the lead, together with the Baron and the Captain, but you have barely covered a quarter of the distance to the hamlet when your tracking senses warn you that a threat is approaching from the north.

If you wish to insist they return to the river, turn to **96**.
If you wish to hurry towards the hamlet, turn to **225**.

295

Before the door closed you caught sight of a map spread out across a trestle table in the centre of the cabin. You whisper to Prarg what you have seen, then you tell him to wait for you here while you try to get a closer look at that map. It may contain a clue to Magnaarn's whereabouts.

Slowly you work your way across the snowy ground towards the ditch which encircles the camp. Your camouflage skills keep you from being seen by the Drakkarim sentries and you are able to reach the cover of this shallow, ice-filled trench with little difficulty. While you wait here for the chance to make a dash for the cabin, you notice two points of entry: the main door and a side window.

If you wish to enter the cabin by the door, turn to **265**.
If you choose to enter through the side window, turn to **15**.

296

Breathless from the fight, you step away from the slain beast and wipe its foul blood from your weapon before sheathing it in your belt. A distant howl echoes along the tunnel, a chilling cry that warns you that the creature you have just defeated was not the only one of its kind.

Fearful of staying a moment longer, you turn around and hurry along the tunnel. Before long you find yourself in a section of this underground labyrinth which has suffered greatly during the recent rockfalls. Many fissures have opened up the stone floor and shattered the walls, but you take these obstacles in your stride and soon arrive at a ruined staircase which ascends to a landing. Here you are confronted by the corpse of a Drakkarim guard. It is slumped beside a mound of rubble which is blocking the stairs to the next level above. A quick examination of the dead body reveals that both arms are broken. Injured and trapped here by the rockfall, it appears that this guard eventually died of thirst.

If you wish to search the body further, turn to **269**.
If you wish to attempt to clear away the rubble that is blocking the stairs, turn to **16**.

297

Drawing on your mastery, you will the creature to cease its mental attack. It hesitates, but not for long. Its instincts quickly overcome your psychic commands and, with a terrifying howl, it leaps forward and attacks.

Turn to **267**.

298

You utter the words of the Brotherhood spell "Lightning Hand" and point your index finger at the trio of Drakkarim. A surge of crackling energy gushes from your hand and explodes in their midst, scattering them like rag dolls. Their comrades flee the wagon and, without slowing, you gallop through the gap in the barricade with barely inches to spare and race along the road beyond. You have passed successfully through the inner defensive line, but, as Prarg quickly points out, you have yet to reach the outer defences of Shugkona.

Turn to **28**.

299

You exit this chamber by the archway and discover yet another flight of stairs awaiting you. At first you bemoan the thought of another long and weary climb, but then you detect something which quickly changes your mind. You can smell clean, fresh air descending this stairwell.

You hurry up the stairs, spurred on by the wintery chill which grows steadily colder as you ascend. You count one hundred steps before you arrive at a small chamber which is heaped with rubble. Its only door is blocked by debris and huge slabs of shattered marble, making an immediate exit impossible. But it is not the door which commands your attention; it is a narrow circular shaft which is set into the middle of the ceiling. It is the source of the cold, wintery draft.

Expectantly, you step closer and investigate this shaft. For the most part it is dark, but you can see glimmers of grey daylight far above, and you can hear the whistling of the wind. But you can also hear another sound, one that is quite unexpected. It is a buzzing, insectile noise. You focus upon the darkness and suddenly you see that the noise comes from nests of winged insects which are fixed along the inside of the shaft.

If you possess Grand Pathsmanship, and have reached the rank of Sun Knight, turn to **218**.

If you do not possess this Discipline, or have yet to reach this level of Kai rank, turn to **253**.

300

One of the bolts hits you in the back with such force that you are lifted off your feet. There is a fiery flash of pain, then a terrifying numbness engulfs your body. As you crash face first into the swirling foam, you realize to your horror that you cannot move any of your limbs. The bolt has severed your spine and, in the long minutes which follow, slowly you drown in the tide.

Tragically, your life and your quest end here on Battle Isle.

301

A hundred paces further along the tunnel, you turn a corner and find yourself face-to-face with a ghastly creature. From out of the gloom comes a lumbering hulk with hungry scarlet eyes. This beast is covered with vile fur which glistens in the eerie half-light of the tunnel, and its long sinewy arms are outstretched as if it is sleepwalking. But this beast is not asleep. In both of its huge hands it holds chunks of dagger-like flint which it wields like weapons. Its bloated belly skims the floor as it gathers speed, and a brown gluey saliva runs freely from its fanged lower jaw.

With a shriek, the creature lunges towards you, flailing at the air with its brace of dagger-flints as it closes in for the kill. You are forced to retreat as it comes rushing towards you at a breathtaking pace.

Tunnel Stalker:
COMBAT SKILL 44   ENDURANCE 49

Due to the unexpected speed and ferocity of its attack, reduce your COMBAT SKILL score by 3 points for the first round of this combat only.

If you win this combat, turn to **296**.

302

As one, the soldiers draw their weapons and come rushing towards the ground floor entrance to the grain tower. You retreat from the window and look around for a means of escape for already you can hear the first of the enemy climbing the stairs. With fear running cold in your veins you cross to a window on the far side of the tower. Outside, directly below the window, you see a Drakkar lancer sitting astride a warhorse. His lance is sheathed in a tube-like scabbard fixed to the rear of his saddle, and in his hand he holds aloft a heavy-bladed cavalry sabre. He is staring at the onrushing soldiers and is completely unaware that you are barely a few yards away.

Swiftly you climb on to the window ledge, draw your weapon, and leap on to the unwary lancer below.

Pick a number from the *Random Number Table*. If you possess Grand Huntmastery, add 3 to the number you have picked.

If your total score is now *4* or less, turn to **139**.
If your total score is now *5* or more, turn to **26**.

303

The guard crashes to the bottom of the trench, screaming—''Gaz rekenarim! Gaz rekenarim!''

The other Drakkarim are slow to react, and only one manages to snatch up his spear in his defence as you come leaping over the parapet. He thrusts it at your head and you dodge aside just in time to avoid a fatal wound, yet the tip gouges your shoulder: lose 2 ENDURANCE points.

"Sarnac and Lencia!" cries Prarg, as side-by-side you land in the trench and strike out at its defenders. Your attack is swift and deadly. In less than five seconds, you have dispatched all four of the Drakkarim trench-troopers who occupy this position, over-coming three of them before they could even unsheathe their swords.

Keen to maintain your advantage of surprise, you quickly leave the trench and rush across the remaining strip of open ground which separates you from the town's outlying dwellings. Prarg points ahead to an alleyway that lies sandwiched between two burntout hovels, and immediately you follow as he hurries to-wards its shadowy entrance.

Turn to **162**.

304

You conjure forth the Brotherhood spell of "Lightning Hand" and, at once, your right arm is sheathed with rings of glowing blue-fire. Calmly you raise your hand, point your index finger at the leader of the Akataz pack, and with a blink of your eyes you launch a crackling pulse of energy directly at his head. The bolt arcs through the cold air and hits the war-dog squarely between the eyes, sending it tumbling backwards in a flurry of snow to disappear among the trees.

Instantly the others halt in their tracks, visibly shaken. You sense that the pack is torn now between its desire to satisfy its gnawing hunger and its natural instinct for survival. Eventually the instinct for self-preservation wins out, and one by one the dogs turn and flee for the safety of the Tozaz forest.

Confident that the Akataz will not be back this night, you return to the boat to catch some sleep while Prarg begins his turn on guard.

Turn to **194**.

305

After several minutes you notice a ledge which juts out from the chasm wall. It is located fifty feet or so directly above the place where you are currently standing. Close to this ledge you see a dark shadow. It marks the entrance to another tunnel, one that hopefully may lead all the way to the surface.

With renewed optimism, you recite the words of the Brotherhood spell—"Levitation"—and at once you feel gravity losing its grasp. Assisted by this magic, you climb the rough chasm wall with ease and quickly reach the ledge above. Here you cancel the spell before hurrying into the new tunnel in search of a clear route to the surface.

Turn to **59**.

306

Shocked by the death of their leader, the few remaining enemy turn tail and flee across the open plain in panic, with the stinging cheers of their foes echoing in their ears.

Then the cheering is cut short when an ominous noise comes rolling across the plain from the city of Darke. It is a thunderous boom that shakes the very ground on which you stand. You look towards the city and see that the battle is growing ever fiercer. But now there is a new and sinister aspect. Flickerings of magical fire can be seen dancing along battlements, engulfing friend and foe alike. You sense that it is the work of Magnaarn; he and his Nadziranim allies are responsible for this.

Then, through the smoke of battle, you see a Lencian flag flying proudly amidst the carnage that is taking place on the coastal plain, to the south of the city. Here, King Sarnac's crusaders have turned an enemy flank and are storming its weakened center. Maquin and Schera see the flag and, encouraged by their own victory, they decide to march at once in support of the crusader's brave attack.

You wish them both good fortune, for you know the time has come to part company with these brave men. Their destiny awaits them on the field of battle; yours will be found inside the city of

Darke itself where, if you are to fulfil your quest, you must confront Warlord Magnaarn. You bid them farewell and watch as they lead their men in a marching column along the river road towards the field of battle. When they are a mile distant, you set off alone across the plain towards the hamlet, which lies en route to the gates of Darke.

Turn to **140**.

307

There is a loud bang and a great grey cloud billows from the muzzle of the musket. It startles the horse, but you swiftly control the animal and urge it forwards, out on to the road. In the confusion you make your escape northwards, hidden from the eyes of your pursuing enemy by the acrid cloud of gunpowder smoke.

Your ears are ringing but otherwise you and Prarg escape unharmed. The mare is strong and surefooted, and despite the snow, you quickly cover more than eight miles before you encounter something on the road ahead that brings you immediately to a standstill.

Turn to **97**.

308

With weapons drawn you wait for the boat to strike the frost-covered raft of weeds. An unnatural silence has descended upon the surrounding mire, as if every creature of the Hellswamp were holding its breath in anticipation, waiting for the trap to be sprung. The bow grazes the obstruction and suddenly the silence is torn apart by a gurgling screech. Like sorcery-conjured demons, a dozen ghoulish creatures rise up from the murky depths of the swamp amid a seething froth of bubbles. Swiftly they climb from beneath the weed-raft and slink from hiding places along the bank. Within seconds they have you surrounded.

''Ciquali!'' growls Prarg, naming these ghoulish foes. He moves forward, sword raised, and lashes out at the first of these dome-headed creatures as it tries to climb aboard. His razor-sharp blade severs its forearm at the wrist, sending a scaly webbed hand spin-

A dozen ghoulish creatures rise up from the murky
depths of the swamp amid a seething froth of bubbles.

ning into the swamp, trailing green ichor. The beast screams and falls over the side, yet no sooner has it vanished beneath the surface when two more of its kin attempt to haul themselves into the boat.

If you have a Bow and wish to use it, turn to **164**.
If you do not, or choose not to use it, turn to **6**.

309

Quickly you search through the clutter of boxes which lie scattered all around this cabin, and you discover the following which may be of use to you during your mission:

2 potions of Laumspur (each restores 4 ENDURANCE points)
Hourglass
Signet Ring
Bow
3 Arrows
Sword
Brass Key
Dagger

If you decide to keep any of the above, remember to make the necessary adjustments to your *Action Chart*.

To continue, turn to **251**.

310

Prarg is soon paralysed by the intense cold. He ceases all movement when his body goes into shock and rapidly he disappears beneath the water. You rush to help him, approaching as near to the edge of the hole as you dare, and then you see his face pressed to the underside of the ice, close to where you are standing. His eyes are wide open and a stream of bubbles are trailing from his nose and mouth. You must act quickly if you are to save him.

If you wish to jump into the gaping hole in the ice and attempt to pull him out, turn to **85**.
If you decide to attempt to smash another hole in the ice, close to where he is trapped, turn to **216**.

311

With stoic determination you begin the laborious task of clearing away the rock and rubble which fills this stairwell. You are fearful that it may take you several days to reach the next level, and so it comes as a welcome surprise when, after just a few minutes work, you see a gap appearing at the top of the mound. A gust of cold, wintery air wafts through this breach, rekindling your hopes of reaching the surface. Revived by the cold clean air, you attack the rubble with renewed vigour. But then your hopes are shaken when you hear a sinister sound; behind you, something is climbing the stairs to the landing.

If you possess Kai-alchemy, and have reached the rank of Sun Knight or higher, turn to **232**.

If you do not possess this Discipline, or have yet to reach this level of Kai training, turn to **257**.

312

The tip of your lance penetrates the Death Knight's armoured breastplate and kills him instantly. The force of the blow is such that it snaps the lance in two and nearly knocks you clean out of your saddle, but you manage to hold tight and quickly you recover. Moments later you reach the platform to see Captain Prarg struggling to break free from his gaolers. He succeeds and he comes running towards you. With a yell he leaps from the platform and lands astride the rump of your horse.

"Go, Lone Wolf, go!" he shouts, excitedly.

You dig your heels into the horse's flanks and take off through the confused mass of Drakkarim towards an avenue on the north side of the square. Prarg's hands are still tied behind his back and in order to stop himself from falling off the horse, he is forced to hang on to your cloak with his teeth.

You gallop out of the square and along the northern avenue which is flanked by barracks and hovels. Arrows come whistling from their windows but they are poorly aimed and fly wide of their mark. You glance over your shoulder and see that some Drakkarim horsemen are grouping up at the exit from the square in order to give chase. You urge the horse onwards, and as you speed towards a distant corner, you use your Magnakai skill of Nexus to loosen Prarg's bonds. Minutes later you turn the corner and see the road which leads out of Shugkona. Your spirits rise, but they are quickly dashed when you see that your route of escape is blocked.

Turn to **20**.

313

As your slain enemies keel over backwards and splash into the mire, you roll Prarg on to his back then watch as the remaining Ciquali, now leaderless, turn away and disappear as quickly as they had come, slipping back to the cold, dark safety of their hiding places beneath the surface. Silence returns, and for a long moment you stay alert, suspecting trickery, then slowly you relax; they have gone.

Aided by your healing skills, Prarg makes a speedy recovery from the battering he sustained in combat with the Ciquali chieftain. The boat, too, has survived the attack and you are able to continue without further delay. As soon as you pass the obstruction, you hoist the sail and catch the prevailing wind which propels you northwards along the channel beyond.

You are hungry after your encounter. Unless you possess Grand Huntmastery, you must now eat a Meal or lose 3 ENDURANCE points.

To continue, turn to **98**.

314

The moment you strike your killing blow, the Nyras Sceptre explodes with a brilliant flash and you are knocked down by the sudden release of energy. For several minutes you lie unconscious on the floor of this wind-swept turret, until you are found and revived by your guide and companion, Captain Prarg. Nothing remains of either Warlord Magnaarn or the Nyras Sceptre; both have been utterly destroyed. Prarg helps you to your feet, and as you look out across the battle-torn landscape, you witness a wondrous event. The Gulf of Lencia is dotted with scores of square-rigged men o' war. They are the ships of the Kasland fleet: at last Lencia's allies have arrived.

Thanks to your bravery and determination, the power which has so devastated this land is now no more. The destruction of the Nyras Sceptre heralds a turning of the tides of war in the west. The Nadziranim and their armies flee the field of battle and are pursued by the allies all the way back to their strongholds in the north. The remnants of Magnaarn's army is routed and swept out of Nyras and, after many centuries, this country finally returns to its rightful heirs.

In recognition of your victory over Warlord Magnaarn, King Sarnac of Lencia and Archduke Chalamis of Kasland hold a royal banquet in Vadera in your honour. You are heaped with praise and you receive the thanks and warm congratulations of a grateful populace.

Well done, Lone Wolf. Once again you have achieved a victory over the forces of darkness and proved yourself to be worthy of the title "Kai Grand Master." Yet the fight against Evil goes ever on. On your return to your homeland you will be faced with a new and deadly challenge that will test your remarkable skills and unquestionable bravery. The nature of this challenge can be found in the next Grand Master adventure, which is entitled:

THE LEGACY OF VASHNA

RANDOM NUMBER TABLE

8	7	6	1	3	5	6	8	6	2
0	8	3	5	0	5	8	7	4	1
9	5	1	2	5	7	4	6	1	8
5	8	4	7	6	5	8	6	0	9
0	1	9	4	2	9	0	3	1	4
5	8	1	4	3	2	7	0	8	5
1	8	6	7	8	0	2	3	5	0
6	2	0	3	4	9	8	6	2	9
2	4	8	7	6	5	2	1	0	6
4	6	5	2	9	0	1	4	8	7